from e to you

What would you do when your dad suggests you e-mail his best friend's daughter, and the girl turns out to be as feisty as a crocodile with a few sore teeth? This is the fate that befalls Guy Woodham. Little does he know when he starts mailing Annabelle that his quiet and slightly unhappy life is about to be stirred up with a whole heap of trouble.

Created jointly by popular authors Linda Newberry and Chris d'Lacey this book is written entirely as e-mails. Somewhat unexpectedly Chris writes Annabelle's voice and Linda pretends to be a teenage boy. This book is funny, moving and ludicrous by turns.

Other books by Chris d'Lacey

The Fire Within – *Orchard*
Pawnee Warrior – *Random House*
Ice Fire – *Orchard*
Fly Cherokee Fly – *Transworld*
Falling for Mandy – *Random House*
The Snail Patrol – *Barn Owl Books*
The Salt Pirates of Skegness – *Orchard*
Riverside United – *Transworld*

Other books by Linda Newbery

The Shell House – *David Fickling Books*
The Damage Done – *Scholastic*
Flightsend – *Scholastic*
No Way Back – *Orchard*
Break Time – *Orchard*
Some Other War – *Barn Owl Books*
Sisterland – *David Fickling Books*

Chris d'Lacey   Linda Newbery

from e to you

Barn Owl Books

Originally published by Scholastic in 2000
This edition published in 2004 by Barn Owl Books
157 Fortis Green Road, London N10 3LX
Barn Owl Books are distributed by Frances Lincoln,
4 Torriano Mews, Torriano Avenue, London NW5 2RZ

ISBN 1-903015-35-9

Designed and typeset by Douglas Martin Associates, Oadby
Printed and bound in Great Britain by
Creative Print and Design Wales, Ebbw Vale

Linda > I've got a great idea for a book!

Chris > (yawn) What about?

Linda > Boy and a girl meeting by e-mail.

Chris > Hmm. What's the plot?

Linda > There isn't one . . . yet.

Chris > Why are you telling me?

Linda > I want YOU to be the girl.

HELLO

Dear Annabelle,

Hi, my name's Guy. In case you've never heard of me, I'm sending this because my Dad and your Dad think we ought to be e-mail pen-pals. I bet you've got far better things to do than write to a boy you've never even met who lives about a hundred miles away near the Welsh border, so I won't mind if you don't want to bother.

Best wishes,
Guy

NAME, RANK & CEREAL NUMBER

Dear woodham@woodworks.com,

You're right, I've never heard of you. Or your dad. Do you like Choco Pops? I'm spooning my way through a bowlful at the moment. Its my dad's turn to make the tea and feed the dog tonight, and he's forgotten – again. I am therefore ravenous (and a little tetchy).

Anyway, regarding:
> I bet you've got far better things to do than write
> to a boy you've never even met.

Right again, sort of. If I do not faint with hunger I am about to go swimming with my friend Laura Blackman, and later I am going to get on with my novel. However, as this is clearly a Dad thing and

I will get hassled by He Who Must Be Obeyed now that She Who Must Be Obeyed has gone on her dig, I will add you to my list of things to do and might write to you again at the weekend.

Is your dad the one who invents the ice-cream flavours?

Yours, Annabelle, only daughter of your dad's friend.

PS Your name's got to go. You surely can't expect me to write "H Guy" at the beginning of a letter? I mean, yuk. It rhymes! Everybody knows that poetry is pants.

GUY BITING BACK

Dear Annabelle,

You've got some cheek, starting off by having a go at my name. I'm not changing it just for you. There are plenty of famous Guys who were quite happy with it – Guy Gibson, Guy Fawkes and Guy the Gorilla for starters. But how many famous Annabelles can you think of? And if I were you I'd drop the last two letters unless you want to be mistaken for a Sindy doll. I picture you as tall and slim with long blonde hair and blue eyes – am I right?

Some queries.

1. Your Mum's dig? Does she have an allotment or something?

2. Getting on with your novel? What, writing one? Or just reading one and trying to be pretentious?

3. Poetry is pants? What do you have against poetry? Or pants?

About ice-cream flavours, I haven't a clue what you're on about. Are you mixing my Dad up with someone else's? Mine's an accountant. BORING. That's how he knows your Dad. Anyway, we've made enough effort to keep both Dads happy now. We can tell them we tried but we just didn't have anything in common.

Bye, Guy

ARE YOU CALLING ME A BIMBO OR WHAT?!

Hi *Guy*,

Oh yuk! Pass me the bucket, purlease. I do believe I am going to Hughie. Oh gosh, all over my Sindy doll, too. Shame. Now I will not be able to play Houses of Parliament with her tonight and blow her up along with your namesake. Does that answer your question about my appearance? For what it is worth, I have tried to picture you. I see you as small, yellow and incredibly furry. A sort of Guy the Gerbil type. But I digress.

For someone who does not think we have much in common you ask an awful lot of questions. I have put this down to the fact that I am probably the most interesting person in your life right now. But even I cannot bear to leave you dangling, so here are some answers . . .

1. My mum is an archaeologist, clever clogs, which means she likes to dig up bones. Our dog, Ginger, also likes to dig up bones. Strangely, Mum never takes the smelly old mutt with her, which means yours truly has to walk him every night.

2. I am ignoring question 2 on the grounds that it would be pointless trying to explain the concept of creativity to a small furry object. However, you will have guessed from my response that I am *writing* a novel. It is absolutely brilliant. My English teacher, Ms Spence, says I have an "unfathomably exceptional imagination". So there. My dad has tons of books in his study. I am currently reading *Animal Farm*, which is probably where you should be.

3. You have already discovered what effect poetry has on me (see paragraph 1). As for pants, I have nothing against them - except short ones. Are you out of them yet?

Bye, *Guy*
Annabelle with the XTRA letters

OVER AND OUT

Dear Annabelle,

There's no point in this. You obviously haven't got

the slightest interest in anyone except yourself.

Yours sincerely,
Guy Woodham

HOT WATER AND BOTTLES

Dear Guy Woodharn,

There, I was *nice* to you. Despite this:

> You obviously haven't got the slightest interest in
> anyone except yourself.

Cheek! I will have you know that I am actually interested in LOADS of people, especially Rodeo Ronson who plays lead guitar with Forged Metal. I've got a bus ticket with half his autograph on. It is in my special mementoes box, *thank you*.

And please DO NOT SEND ANY MORE MESSAGES TO MY DAD'S E-MAIL ADDRESS because HE gets to them first. *Total embarrassment*. I have made him give me my own address. All future grumpy remarks should now be sent to: **annabelle©dragonfire.violet.com** and you are in major trouble if you forget.

I expect you're wondering why I'm even *bothering* writing to you again? It's because *you* have got *me* into a LOT of trouble. My dad asked how we were getting on yesterday and I had to tell him you DUMPED me. Do you know what he said? "What did you do to upset him, Annabelle?" As if it was all my fault! He says I have got to try again because we might be "good for one another" and if I don't he will dock 50p from my spending money this week! "Try telling him something about yourself" he said. Excuse me? I think it should be the other way round. I have already told you loads of things and you have not answered any of my questions.

So, I live in Oxford, city of dreaming spires, and when I grow up I would like to travel the world and meet people (yawn). I also have a transparent hot water bottle with plastic fish swimming inside it. When I fall asleep with my feet on top of it I sometimes dream that the fish are tickling my toes. (I can't believe I'm saying this, but it's got to be worth fifty pence of *any*body's money.)

Your turn,
Annabelle King (Miss)

PS For what it's worth I'm sorry I had a go at your name, OK?

HAPPY CHRISTMAS – NOT

Dear Annabelle,

If you're planning to use me as a way of staying in favour with your Dad, you're going to have to try harder than this. But why's he bullying you to keep mailing? Is he hoping you might learn something about communicating with people?

About answering your questions – I can't remember you asking any. I trashed your extremely tedious messages as soon as I'd read them, so there's no way of checking.

Since you ask (huh! some chance) I've just had the worst Christmas of my life. I hope yours was better.

Guy

SORRY SANTA STORY

Dear Grrr,

I'm sorry, I cannot write your name because every time it comes into my head I just want to growl. Grrr! There. I thought of you again. I told my dad exactly what you said, and do you know what? – he chuckled! So I hid his TV remote control and that got him hopping (and I don't mean channels). Now he says he is going to dock 50p from my pocket money every WEEK until I start to talk to you nicely! When I stamped my foot and asked him why, he said it was for my "spiritual development". Help! I am living with a New Age dad! (And a smug one at that.)

So, Grrr, why was your Christmas so miserable? Did Santa get stuck in your chimney or something? I bet you still believe in him, don't you? Tough. I can prove he doesn't exist. Anyway, your Christmas story surely can't be as bad as the time I queued to see Santa at Merriman's grotto and he had run out of presents so he sang me a song? His beard had gravy stains down it as well and he burped every time he went Ho, Ho, Ho. I still have nightmares about it. So there.

Yours, quite nicely, with teeth only slightly gritted,
Annabelle

PS The song was *Give A Little Whistle*.

MY WORST CHRISTMAS

Dear Guy,

Notice, I didn't growl. There, I have told you something else about myself, namely that I don't stay mad at people for long. Come on, Guy. Talk to me. Please. I wasn't ever mad at you really. I was just a bit annoyed because I thought you thought I was a stupid soppy girly. Now you know I am really quite "zesty". Well, that's what Mum says, anyway. "More zest than a lemon", she says I've got. And lemons can be a bit sharp, can't they?

Come on, Fair's fair. I don't tell my Santa story to everyone, you know. I certainly wouldn't tell it to Tracey Scudding, and she is supposed to be my second-best friend. Claw. Claw. I think you should definitely write and tell me about your miserable Christmas. I know you want to tell *someone* or you wouldn't have mentioned it in the first place. One night, last week, I couldn't sleep and I tried to think about the worst Christmas I'd really had. It was only last year actually. Dad took my cat, Hornbeam, to the vet and he had a growth under his tongue (Hornbeam, not the vet). I wasn't sad that Hornbeam had to be put to sleep because he couldn't eat properly and would have starved; I was sad because Dad cried when he told me the bad news. Oh no, now I have dripped a tear on to the keyboard just thinking about it. Sorry, keyboard.

You had better write back or I will be having sleep-less nights for ever. I will also be penniless (no pocket money, remember) and playing spoons on the streets. Did I tell you I could play the spoons? It comes in quite handy at Christmas parties – oops, there's that word again. Please write back. I promise if you tell me your Christmas story I will give the next 50p that Dad would have docked to the charity of your choice.

Your could-be friend,
Annabelle

ZESTY OR PESTY?

Dear Annabelle,

Thanks for your two e-mails. My Christmas was the worst ever because it was the first one without my Mum.

I'm sorry about your cat. But at least cats get put to sleep when it's obvious they're going to die.

My Dad cried too. Back then.

More cheerful topic: I've been away over New Year, with my friend and his Dad, climbing the Three Peaks in the Yorkshire Dales. In case you haven't heard of them,they're called Ingleborough, Whernside and Pen-y-Ghent. There was snow and ice and it was brilliant! (You won't be impressed. I don't expect you to be. You've probably climbed Everest and K2 without oxygen.)

Happy New Year!

Best wishes,
Guy

NEW YEAR BLUES

Oh Guy! How could you? Now you have made me feel really awful. Here's me going on about losing Hornbeam, and all the time you . . . well, I can't even bear to type it. I want to type something appropriate and sensitive and all I can think of is writing about the time my mum went away to Egypt last year, studying the tomb of some ancient king, and I missed her horribly and Dad said "Mary?" every time the phone rang and it was never her.

Oh no, I have just realized that I have been writing about graves (groan). I suppose I *could* go back and wipe it all out, but if I leave it in perhaps it will prove that I can be sincere. I am really, really sorry about your mum. At least I still have one. Digging. Somewhere.

I'm glad your New Year was good and exciting. It might surprise you to know that I am actually a snow and ice sort of person. I hate the summer because my freckles come out. So I usually walk around in a big floppy hat. It's cool (both meanings!) and it shadows my face. I have never been to Yorkshire but if I do I will be sure to keep a look out for your peaks. Three. They shouldn't be too hard to spot. Are you going to climb more? Does this mean you are tough and rugged? Have you done a Duke of Edinburgh thingy? My Uncle Glenn did one of those. He was in something called the Mountain Rescue Service. Though I don't know how you rescue a mountain. OK. Bad joke. And talking of mountains never mind oxygen, you would not get me up Everest if Forged Metal were playing their last gig there and they desperately wanted someone to play the spoons. I am terrified of heights. I once had a fight with Gina Potterton at school because she wanted to see what I looked like in her platforms. I had to pretend they were utterly pants because I knew if I put them on I would start to wobble and then I might faint. It wasn't too bad. I only lost one big clump of hair and you should have seen the scratches on her scrawny neck. Sorry, I'm twittering on a bit, aren't I?

The only exciting thing that happened to me over New Year was that Jupiter, my guinea pig, escaped from his cage. I call him Jupiter because he's round and fat. I nearly put a red felt spot on him once but it wouldn't stick to his tufty fir. Anyway, we looked everywhere for him. I was sure he'd gone under the floorboards, but Dad said he was far too piggy for that and had probably "popped down to the shops for some chocolate". He's crackers, my dad. Then one day last week we heard this blipping sound under the floor in my room. Dad said it was just the pipes, but I wailed and said it was Jupiter's tummy going mad for food. Dad cracked. He had the carpet, the underlay and the floorboards up – and guess what? He was right all along it was just the pipes gurgling away. And we didn't find Jupiter either, but we did find – oops, gotta go. D coming.

A

MUMS, HAMSTERS AND D

Dear Annabelle,

Was that mean, or was that mean? Breaking off like that? Why didn't you finish after D had gone? Who is D? Darth Vader? Damon Hill? or possibly just Dad? And if so, why did that mean you had to stop?

What did you find under the floorboards? And where's Jupiter? He must be ravenous by now if you still haven't found him. Couldn't you poke sunflower seeds down between the floorboards? I had a hamster once (no, not a gerbil) and it used to get out and hide behind the radiators and chew up bits of carpet for a nest, so I can sympathize with him. And even perhaps with you.

I've discovered that we have things in common after all.You're an only child and so am I. We both have absent mothers. My Mum's name was Mary, too. Odd, isn't it? Because there can't be that many Marys about. I mean, I don't know any others. And she had freckles, my Mum.

By the way, Dad's bought this digital camera thing and I've worked out how to download images on to the computer (and then I had to show *him* how – he's useless with technology) so now I can send you a picture! It's me, Mark and Mark's Dad. We're not actually on top of Pen-y-Ghent – we're in our back garden with all our gear. So – guess which one is me! And I know you'll say the tubby, balding one in the middle, so don't – that's Mark's Dad. In answer to your question, no, I'm not what you'd call rugged or tough, but I am doing the Duke of Edinburgh award (silver this year) and I do have a sort of obstinacy (according to Mum) that sends me up mountains whenever I get the chance. Mark and I are going to do Ben Nevis next. On our own, without his Dad. Don't forget to let me know about Jupiter.

Best wishes,
Guy

WAITING FOR LAURA

Dear G,

That's you, by the way. I don't mean Goldilocks or Godzilia, do I? Of course D stands for Dad, dummy. Darth Vader! I ask you. He would hardly come clumping up our stairs, would he? I could finish my novel in the time it would take him to climb three flights and peek darthly over my shoulder. I'd be able to hear him wheezing a mile off. He's got a very bad chest, hasn't he, DV?

Anyway, please pay attention cos I don't have long at the keyboard tonight. Dad wants to print out some lecture notes and Laura is calling round for me soon. We're going to Gina Potterton's house to watch a video – *The Last of the Mohicans*. Gina's big sister, Tara, bought it in a sale at the video shop. She says it's a TMS (total must-see). A croaky old film about Red Indians? Zzz. Get real. At least Gina's mum keeps loads of choccy ice-cream in her fridge. I might demand pop-corn as well tonight as I'll probably be bored right out of my skull.

Yawn. On to more interesting stuff. The reason I had to cut off sharpish last time is because I didn't want Dad to see my message. The thing that was secreted under our floorboards appears to be of a highly sensitive nature. It is so HS that he who must be obeyed went WHITE when he saw it. He also gets snappy if I talk about it. It might have been de-mail not e-mail if he had caught me writing to you about it. So I wasn't going to take any chances. The worst of it is, I don't properly know what the mysterious face-paling thingy is. And its driving me MAD with bogglement. I am so horribly boggled my ankles are itching. My freckles are coming out early as well. This is serious. Grr! Grr! GRRRR!

I wouldn't mind, but I was the first to see it, too. While Dad was busy getting splinters in his fingers, ripping up the boards near Jupiter's cage, I spotted a bit of loose carpet in a corner and tugged it back. Underneath was a small board without any nails in. Stupidly, I said "Dad, why don't we look under this board, here?" He gave me one of his frazzled looks. I held the board up to show him. His face went a funny sort of purple colour. So I did my very best little girly grin and glanced in the hole, hoping to see Jupiter's nose and whiskers – I saw the thingy instead. INCREDIBLY STUPIDLY (for me) I said: "Dad, what's this?" and reached into the dustiness and picked the thingy out. It was loosely wrapped in a satiny blue cloth. It felt about as heavy as a good-sized pebble, but flatter and sort of triangular-shaped. Dad came across the room as I started to unwrap it. I got as far as, "Gosh, it looks like a –" when he stuck out his hand and said "Annabele, give that to me. Now, please."

Really tight and snappy – and parental. "I found it,"

I said. Then he really popped. “NOW, please!”

You could almost see the steam puffing out of his ears. So I had no choice but to hand the thingy over. He took one quick look then wrapped it again and shoved it in his pocket. “Well, is it a locket in your pocket?” I said, more pouty than cheeky. He turned away, stroking his beard (like he does). “Annabelle, go to your room,” he said, which just proves he’s barmy cos we were already IN my room! “Well, go to another room, then!” he snapped. So I stomped off and sat on the loo for an hour. “You’d better find Jupiter NOW!” I shouted. And he must have tried really hard as well because he was banging and clattering about for ages. My room was a horror zone when he’d finished, furniture and cupboards everywhere. And Mum says *I* always leave it in a mess! And he *still* hadn’t found Jupiter, and he *still* wouldn’t say what the thingy really was or what it was doing there or who it belonged to. But I’m sure it was a locket. It was silvery and had a chain attached. It looked quite precious. But who does it belong to? And what was it doing under my boards? And where is it *now*? (Dad’s hidden it somewhere.) Fear not, I’m on the trail.

Flipping heck, Guy, this is squammy! I have just done a word count on the story of the thingy and it came to 567words. That’s more than I wrote on my novel all last week. And I haven’t even told you my other Dad news yet. Might as well as Laura is late.

At breakfast the other day, while Dad was eating a bowl of soggies, he asked how you and I were getting on now. “Fandabidozi,” I told him. “Good,” he said (dribbling milk). “I expect you’ll be wanting a rise in pocket money, then?” Wow, talk about Christmas! (Well, you know what I mean.) I couldn’t decide if he was bribing me to keep on writing to you or just feeling guilty about the locket but I wasn’t going to look a gift dad in the mouth. So I said, "Yes, PLEASE, good kind Daddy!" and he put down his paper and gave me an extra TWO QUID. I was gobsmacked. There is no other word to describe it.

But, here’s the weird bit, the *first* weird bit, anyway. Talking about you made me think about that picture you sent. I printed it out on our super-duper A3 printer. You look quite good blown up to A3. Well, you would if I knew which one was you. (Tease.)

Anyway, I ran upstairs to get the picture and shoved it in front of Dad’s paper. After he’d stopped tutting and clucking about not being able to do the crossword I asked, “Which one do you think is Guy, then?” He glanced at it rather grudgingly at first, then blinked three times and couldn’t seem to take his eyes off it. “Well?” I prompted. He cleared his throat with a nervous cough – and guess what he said? “The tubby, balding one in the middle." (Huh. Quelle surprise.) So I threatened to tug his ear hairs out if he didn't come up with a sensible answer. He huffed and puffed a bit then said. "Well, which one would you *like* it to be?"

And I pointed . . . oh no, this could be terrible, but it's all your fault for giving me a choice. I'm sorry if you are the one with the teeth on the right, Guy, but I pointed to the thoughtful-looking one on the left. The one with the shock of dark hair, as Mum would say. "Trust you to go for the handsome one," said Dad. "You're blushing, by the way." So I poked him hard in the ribs and said, "You know, don't you? Have you *seen* Guy, then? I thought it was just his dad you knew?" And do you know what he did? He flipping well SHRUGGED. "The last time I saw Guy was in a pram," he said. "Him, that is, not me. I suppose he could be the one on the left.His mother had . . . dark hair, as I recall." And then he moved the picture away. I s'pose I should have shut up there and then. I mean, he'd already upped my pocket money and given me a sort of clue to the picture. But I couldn't help it. I just blabbed. I said, "I'm glad I've got you, Dad." And he gave me his long hard over-the-glasses look. "What brought that on?" he said. I linked my arm in his. "I feel sorry for Guy; his mum died not long ago." And I swear he shuddered. Honest, I felt his shoulder ripple. "Yes, I know," he said really spookily. Then I put my foot in it big time."Maybe she'll coochy Hornbeam if she sees him?" I said.

And he got up, slammed his paper on the chair, told me not to be so "bloody ridiculous" and would it possibly be too much to ask me not to leave the bathroom tap running in future?

Help. What did I do?! I know he doesn't believe in God and stuff, but there was no need to get like that, was there? I mean – Oops, there's the door-bell. Time to go. Will have to mail you some more tomorrow.

AH, AH, AH, AH, AHHH! That was my Mohican war cry. I'll try that on Dad next time he gets stuffy. (It works on Ginger – he's just hidden behind the door.)

Ciao for now,
Annabellow

ABOUT GOD & STUFF

Dear Annabelle,

I'm glad I survived being blown up (to A3).

I'm supposed to be doing my Geography course work (deadline coming up) but I keep thinking about this instead. A couple of messages ago you asked whether I believed in Santa and said you could prove he doesn't exist. Here's a bigger one: what's the Annabelle view (I bet you've got one) on God? I just can't get this God business. The time when he's let you down most badly is just the time you're expected to start believing in him. I mean, at Mum's funeral. She and Dad never went to church, but suddenly we were all meant to behave as if God was there all the time. Well, if he is, WHY DID HE LET IT HAPPEN?

"How are you coping?" people are always asking us. I'm not even sure what Coping is, but we just sniff heroically and say, "Oh, we're managing." I'm becoming quite an expert at the Heroic Sniff but the problem is it's just an act. And a worse problem is that I think Dad is coping. I mean, it's only six months and he *shouldn't* be, should he?

Top Secret stuff coming up now. You may be wondering how I can say this stuff about Dad when we share an e-mail address. The fact is, I save all my messages on disk and then trash them. Then I hide the disk. So he can't read my messages, but I read all his. At least, any that look interesting.

Best wishes,
Guy

HPS My term starts tomorrow – urggg. Does yours?

PPS Your dad was right to tell you off for leaving the tap running. Water is precious. That's what my Geography project's about.

LIFE, THE UNIVERSE AND DANIEL DAY-LEWIS

Dear Guy,

. . . mmrnm. Don't mind me. Just . . . floating, that's all. Nearly a whole day on and I am still in a swoon over Daniel Day-Lewis (a Mohican, but not the last). Phwooar, what a dish. I take back everything I said. Laura thought he looked "cute", with his feathers and everything, but a bit too "old and crusty" for us. Puh, I thought he was DDG, even if he does pay full on the bus.

OK, now the serious bit. Annabelle's theories on GOD, part one. In the beginning there were ALIENS, I reckon. I think this is the only sensible answer to Life, the Universe and Jupiter's disappearance. Sometimes I think that's what Mum is doing out in Egg-whipped (that's a joke: it's how my dad pronounces Egypt; told you he was barmy): looking for signs of alien intelligence. She is always telling me that the early meringue-makers (egg-whippers; come on, Guy, keep up. Do you cook?) were streets ahead of other civilizations. It can't be coincidence that they worshipped Sun gods and drew pictures of cigar-shaped chariots, can it? Or was that the Incas? History is not my best subject. And yes, our term did start the same day as yours. Boo! We have got a new Maths teacher. His name is Mr Phiggins and he's really funny. Our old teacher, Ms Frith, left to have a baby. Everyone was glad, because she wasn't at all funny. She once made us calculate how long it took ancient Brit man to move those massive stones from Wales to make Stonehenge. As if anyone cares! If you ask me, they were beamed up by alien spaceships and dropped on Salisbury Plain, those stones. I think they were a baby alien monster's building bricks. But this doesn't help about your mum, does it?

I'm sorry, Guy. I don't mean to make fun or hurt your feelings or anything. Honestly, I don't. The truth is, I don't know what to believe. There are so many spiffy things in the world that you have to believe in *something*, don't you? Avril Whylip once asked Ms Spence how God can be in loads of places at once – and where was he now? Ms Spence just said that in her opinion when we are "communing" with nature we are probably "standing next" to God. So perhaps when you are up a mountain one day you will bump into God burning bushes or something. He always seems to be up a mountain in the Bible. High beings like high places, I suppose. Perhaps then you can ask him face to face why he lets all these terrible things happen? I know what you mean about that. The day after Hornbeam died I sobbed, not very heroically, all over Dad's shirt. "Why now, Dad?" I wailed. "Just before Christmas, too? He won't be able to play with the baubles on the tree!" Dad stroked my hair and said there was never a good time to die, petal. I suppose he's right, if you think about it.

I don't mean to pry, G, but if it's not too cheeky will you tell me some more about your mum? What was she like? Was she kind and loving and generally mumsy? Does it help if you talk about her? I couldn't look at another cat for ages after Hornbeam went for his big snooze. But now I just remember all the fun times we had and feel warm inside when I talk about him. Perhaps your dad feels the same about your mum. Or perhaps he's just good at hiding his emotions and you're . . . well, not. Tell me if you like. I'll be nice. Promise.

Gotta go in a minute. Dad's just shouted that my tea is on the table. It smells like char-grilled burgers again. Mind you, beans on toast smells like char-grilled burgers the way Dad does it. He's not exactly the world's best chef. I keep leaving *Can't Cook, Won't Cook* on the telly for him, but he just flips over to watch *University Challenge* and shout abuse at Jeremy Paxman. Oh yeah, and don't worry about him snooping through your letters to me. I've got a password on my e-mail address which he wouldn't guess in a zillion years – TAMPON! Our secrets are safe. No worries.

He's calling me again so I will end by saying I looked for the locket all afternoon while he was out at rugby. It wasn't in any of his normal hiding-places (stamp!) so there is something mega-important about it. I have GOT to find it. I'll go and check in the cellar tomorrow. Think of me and my char-grilled throat.

Bye for now,
Annababble

PS Isn't it funny that your mum's name was Mary and she had freckles? My mum hasn't got a single speck. She says she has sand-blown skin (all that sheltering from desert storms, I suppose). She's tough, my mum, and often absent – unlike my dad, who's soft, always here, but absent-minded!!

PPS My tea is going cold, apparently.

PPPS GOOD!

HERE I AM

Hah! I bet THAT surprised you. I downloaded this off Dad's desktop. This will teach you to send me teasy photographs. It's something called a video clip. Dad uses it as a screensaver. He says you need your media viewer to play it (don't ask me).

A

PS This message is about a zillion words shorter than the last one!

WONKY VICAR

Dear Annabelle,

Thanks for babble and video clip. First – have you found any more clues to the Puzzle of the Floorboards? (Or found poor old Jupiter? – I hope he's got large cheek pouches. Perhaps you could leave tempting dishes of lettuce and sunflower seeds around the house, so that he can pop out for a mid-night snack. Hey, you don't think your dog's eaten him, do you?) Your Dad seems to have fallen right out of his tree, but Sherlock Woodham has been hot on the trail, and here are his theories so far.

1. Your Dad doesn't like your Mum being away so often on her digs, so he's planting buried treasure around the house so she can excavate at home instead of slogging away in Egg-whipped.

2. It's a secret present for you. He bought it for you at Christmas but hid it so well that he forgot where it was. Now he's waiting for *next* Christmas.

3. He has a Guilty Secret from his Past. The locket, if it is a locket, is the only remnant of a torrid love affair he had before he met your Mum.

4. The locket contains a key to your real identity which he is planning to reveal to you on your twenty-first birthday. Those lockets often have little pictures in them, don't they? My Mum had one with a piece of my hair in it from when I was a baby. Some of them even have TWO pictures, one on each side of the locket when it's open. That locket shows your real parents, who are descendants of the Russian royal family. Your great-great-grandparents escaped from the Revolution. You are really Anastasia.

About the video clip. I downloaded it and looked at it carefully. First I was disappointed because you're only about three in it and I want to know what you're like *now*. You looked really *sweet* on that pony, and for some odd reason, sweet isn't a word that's ever entered my brain in connection with you. Daft, yes. Motor-mouth, yes. Zesty-pesty, yes. But *sweet* – noooooo! Must be the sharpness of your claws . . . But then something struck me about your Dad, or at least I assume that's your Dad, as he looks all proud and fatherly, and he's hanging on to that furry little pony's reins as if he thinks it might do a Hi-Ho-Silver and throw you off. What dawned on me was that I've seen him before. So I got out my photo album (my Mum made it for me when she knew she was going to die. She put in photos of me from a baby upwards, and some of her and Dad before I was born) – and there he is, your Dad! At least, I'm pretty sure it's him, though at first I thought he was a vicar. The Wonky Vicar Photo is how I think of it, because everyone's tipped up as if they're about to slide right out of the picture. But your Dad's not a vicar, is he? – he doesn't sound like one. And now I look more closely, it's not a dog-collar he's wearing, it's a white roll-neck, under his jacket. And no beard, but then he hasn't got one in your video clip either. Mum's written underneath, "This white bundle has just been launched as Guy Alexander Woodham. Franklin (friend), Dad, me and you - Jane's photo."

(Hey! No mention of your Mum – what if Jane's the Torrid Love Affair!)

So here's the picture for you to see. Is Franklin long for Frank or short for Franklinstein? When he e-mails Dad about his accounts he just puts FMK. When Dad got in I asked him, "You never told me you knew Franklin ages ago. I thought he was someone you know through work." Dad said, "He is, in a way. He's a client. But we go back much farther than that." They met at York, Dad said, when they were students.

I'm not on very good terms with him just now – I'm saving more about that for another e. It was only just now when I started my homework that I thought, wait a minute. If he was such good friends with your Dad, and they're still friends now, how come we've never met?

Anyway, you asked about my Mum. But before I start, I'm glad you liked the pic I sent. To be honest, I really thought you'd prefer Mark and – being honest again – if you had done, I'd have said that was me. Most girls do prefer Mark. If he wasn't such a good mate, I might be jealous. He's far more chatty than I am. I don't know how he does it – he just opens his mouth and things come out. Nothing specially clever or funny, but a lot of girls like it and think he's a great laugh and all that sort of thing. I bet you'd prefer him after all if you met him. You'd out-talk him, no contest.

Mum. Well. After she died I had bereavement counselling. I hated it. There was this youngish guy (no, before you ask, his *name* wasn't Guy) who was OK really but he kept wanting me to talk all the time. That was the whole point of these sessions. To talk. Only I wouldn't. Not to someone, however nice, who was being paid to listen. I got more and more obstinate, with my mouth clammed shut, and he was the one who did all the talking. But if you really want to know . . .

All I can think of is Mum in hospital with her glasses on. That's one of the awful things. She never wore glasses, always contact lenses. Too vain, she said. I only ever saw her with glasses on first thing in the morning or last thing at night. But once she went into hospital, the last time, she never wore her contact lenses again.

And the other thing is that there was a gap in the fence at the end of our garden where one of the wood panels blew down in a gale. We kept saying we'd get it fixed but Dad never got round to it till after Mum died. It may seem a daft thing to think about but I hate it that Mum never saw that mended fence. All those days when Dad and I could have got out there and mended it. Just so she knew. Just so she didn't have to worry about a gap in the fence while she was dying in hospital.

Really she wasn't vain at all. That was her joke. But she could have been. She was one of those people who can do practically anything. She could do *The Times* crossword. Till she got ill she could beat me at tennis, and I don't mean because I'm rubbish, I mean because she was good – she had a fantastic cross-court double-handed backhand. She could speak French and Spanish really well. She knew the Periodic Table and she helped me with an essay on Wilfred Owen and the First World War. I ended up getting an A, but really it was Mum's A. (Yes, I know you think poetry stinks. I used to, once. It's a phase of immaturity you'll probably get over. Ha! Couldn't resist that.)

She was incredibly brave. I know that now. She must have known how ill she was, but for months she tried to pretend it was nothing. It was cancer that killed her, the Big C. For ages she tried to pretend it was small C, but it was big all right. "Just going into hospital for a routine check, nothing to worry about," was all she said. And, "They just want to be absolutely sure." And, "They're just going to try another kind of treatment." *Just* is a word to treat with great suspicion, if you ask me. She was just dying, that was all.

Why did the Big C have to pick on my Mum? Why not someone else? I keep looking at people in the street, thinking: They're alive and healthy and my Mum's dead. Why couldn't the big C have chosen one of them? Yes, I know it's stupid, and unkind because those people are still people even if I don't care about them, but that's what I think.

So now there's *just* me and Dad, and I keep thinking horrible thoughts. Like: How much did he really help her? Because she was putting on a brave show for me, did he fall for it too? Or am I just being incredibly mean, because Dad's the one who's left and I can only see the way he let her down?

My turn for a Mail Marathon. I didn't really mean to go on for so long, especially as I've got two lots of homework (Science, Maths) still to do or I'll get clobbered tomorrow.

Do I cook, you ask. Do I cook? You bet I do, especially now. It's cook or starve, except when my Nan (Dad's Mum) comes over and brings things like home-made steak and kidney pie and treacle pudding with sauce. What I cook is pasta – pasta with everything. Pasta curry? Pasta trifle? Even pasta meringue? I'm your man. Yes, yes, pasta bucket. OK.

Get sleuthing on the locket-and-guinea-pig trail. Hey, perhaps Annabelle and Guy could be a team, like Holmes and Watson, Cagney and Lacey, Morse and Lewis.

Guy

PSSST!

Dear Woodham of the Yard (wood yard, ha!),

Thanks for the wonky pic. I've just downloaded it. More on that in a mo. First, listen closely, there have been *developments*. Yes, with the puzzle of the boards. Print this out, read it, then eat every scrap and flush the loo twice the next day as well. This is MEGA-important stuff. I've got loads of things to tell you but I'm starting with the best bit just in case I have to hit Send fast. Yep, you guessed, Dad Vader is on the prowl again.

Yesterday we had a phone call – from Mum. Ever since the lockety thing turned up, Dad's been trying to get a message to Egg-whipped. He can never call Mum on a dig direct cos she's always under a pyramid or something and can't always get a signal on her mobile. So Dad left a message and Mum called us.

He was in the bathroom when she rang. "Annabelle, can you get that, please?!" he shouted. "It might be your mother." Wo! I was at the phone in a flash! "Hello A," she said. (She always calls me A.) "I don't have long. Is your father there?" She talks like that. "Formal" Dad calls it. "He's on the loo," I said. "Typical," she replied. "How's school? Have you sorted out your exam choices, yet?" Can you believe that? Dead efficient, my mum. She might be calling from halfway round the world but she still knows my complete timetable.

"Mum," I said, "I want to ask you something." There was a crackle – probably a freak sandstorm or something – then she said "If it's about the date for the parents' evening I'll be back before March, don't worry about it." (See what I mean?) "Mum, it's not about school," I said. "I found something under the floor-boards in my room."

Uh oh! Mega-silence. You could have heard one of her mummies yawn. "Put your father on the phone," she said very quietly. (I'm not sure, but I think she sighed.) Suddenly, I heard the toilet flush. "It was silvery," I blabbed. "It looked like a locket." She made a *groaning* noise at that. "Annabelle," she said – and she *never* calls me Annabelle unless she's getting a chin on – "please haul your father off the loo, right now." No way. I bit my lip and went for the big one: Sherlock Woodham's theory number 3. "Mum, is it a remnant of a torrid love affair Dad had before he met you?" There was a sort of splashing noise in the background. I thought she'd fallen in the Nile for a minute. Then I realized it was just her horsey laugh, altered a bit by sand and distance. "Good God, whatever gave you that idea? Your father hasn't done anything torrid for years. Luke-warm, possibly. Go and knock on the bathroom door. Has he disappeared down the plughole or what?" I heard the catch go and knew I had to hurry. "It was my friend," I said. "My e-mail pal suggested it." She humphed and went, "Well, she"s got a jolly good imagination, your e-mail friend.

Where IS your father?" (On the stairs at that point.) "It's not a she, Mum," I blurted. "It's . . . a he. His name's Guy, and his mum died last year."

More silence. I covered the phone slightly and went into a huddle; Dad was just corning into the room. "Annabelle, give me that receiver," he said. But I turned away quickly and the phone fell off the desk and hit him on the toe. While he was hopping round the room I said. "You knew her, didn't you? Her name was Mary, wasn't it? Was she your friend, Mum? Is it her locket? Do you know Guy's dad? Why hasn't anyone talked about Guy before?" Afterwards, of course, I realized this was pathetically stupid, cos she couldn't answer all those things at once. As it happened, she didn't answer any of them. She just sighed and said. "Annabelle, please give the phone to your father." I didn't have to, he'd wrestled it off me by then. I just caught Mum saying, "Franklin, what's going on?" "I could ask you the SAME DAMN THING!" he bellowed.

And then they had an ALMIGHTY ROW. I mean a real house-shaker. "Out!" Dad said, pushing me doorwards. Huh, he wasn't very lukewarm then! Ginger even growled at him. And Ginger doesn't growl at *anything* much. So I sneaked off to listen on the kitchen extension. Guy, I promise, I picked it up as daintily as a fairy, and they both yelled "Annabelle, go to your room!" I slammed the phone down and went. The last thing I heard before I turned up the stairs was Dad shouting: "Well, just how long has this been going on?"

And now I'm worried. What if it's *Mum* who's been having the torrid affair? What if Mum has run away with an Arab sheikh? I bet if I could open that horrible locket there would be a picture of her Egg-whipped lover inside it. I hate that locket. I wish I'd never found it. If I find it again I will lay it on a house brick and smash it to bits.

So that makes two of us who are not exactly on good terms with our dads right now. I feel like printing out that wonky photo, sticking it up on the pinboard in the kitchen and writing, WANTED – FOR LOOKING A PRAT underneath. Maybe I will. He does look weird without his beard. (Oh no, a bit of poetry just snuck up on me!)

Can't remember a time when he didn't have a fuzz. Mum says he has trouble with in-growing hairs. (Perhaps they are worming into his brain? There has to be some explanation for his barminess.) Last year he shaved off half his beard to raise money for the rugby club – and Ginger got spooked and attacked him! It was brilliant. Especialiy when Dad threatened to shave off half Ginger's fur to see how HE liked it – and Ginger bit him! You wouldn't have thought Dad was a vicar then. He "turned the air blue" as my gran likes to say.

Dad's a lecturer at Oxford University. You wouldn't guess it from that photo, though. He looks like a folksinger – or a poet, yuk! I wonder where my mum was? Excavating in the graveyard, probably. And fancy you spotting her nickname for Dad? She calls him Franklinstein when he's in a mood. "Oh, go and bolt another head on, Franklinstein!" she'll shout. She can be rather fierce, my mum. Unlike yours, who I think was probably the sweetest, cleverest, most considerate mum in the whole wide world. Imagine having a mum who wrote essays for you.

Oh Guy, you must miss her so much. I blubbed like mad when you wrote about the fence. It reminded me of Hornbeam again. It used to be my job to clean the cat hairs off his favourite chair. I was still doing it for ages after he died. I kept convincing myself I could still see another one. Then, one night, I realized I couldn't. That night, I just knelt there and started to howl. I buried my face in Hornbeam's cushion and Dad had to come and prize me away. He said, "Come on, petal, you have to let him go." The next night, I didn't clean the chair at all – I sat in it instead, like H would have done. I told him I loved him and missed him like mad, but that I was glad he was free and not in pain any more.

Was your mum in pain? I'm sorry. That's terrible. I shouldn't have asked you that. But I'm going to leave it in because if she was suffering I expect that must be one thing you're glad about: she's not hurting now. And I do think you're being a bit mean to your dad. He did mend the fence after all, didn't he? I think he did it then because he loved her very much and he knew that's what she would have wanted. Can I ask you a great big favour? Will you PLEASE, PLEASE, PLEASE send me an unwonky picture of your mum? I would love to see her, properly, with or without glasses. Please, Guy. I know she's very precious but . . . please?

By the way, I expect you're wondering why I haven't mailed you a picture of me yet? Our scanner has broken. It could be a while before it's fixed, Dad says. I could send you a piccie via snail mail, I suppose, but it wouldn't be the same now, would it?

Better go. Like you, I have homework to do – Mr Phiggins is not so nice after all! If I ever have a snake I will call it Pythonagorus and teach it to swallow my algebra problems. I also have to cook Dad's tea tonight. What's the best way to make pasta really rubbery? He deserves to chew on something the way he's been the last few days.

Bye, keep mailing – and don't forget that image of your mum (pleeze).

A King (as in heart)

PS Ginger would not eat Jupiter, silly. He's terrified of him. When Jupiter spins his wheel it gives Ginger vertigo. Honest. The vet said that. Ginger likes mashed potatoes, anyway. He's not much on meat. I must try him on pasta.

JUPITER UPDATE!!

Drama! Jupiter has been spotted! (And I don't mean next to Saturn, either.) He is on the loose in the garden somewhere. This morning I heard a terrible scream and ran outside to see what it was. I was a bit surprised to see Mrs Swanley, our next-door neighbour, hanging off her trellis arch! I was tempted to ask if she was practising the parallel bars for the next Olympics (she does a lot of keep-fit, Mrs Swanley). It was the way she screamed "LADDERS!" that made me realize something was wrong.

Apparently, she had been up a pair of step ladders, pruning her witch hazel (probably making a new broom), when she had seen a RAT "scampering about" on our lawn. The shock had made her lose her balance and kick the steps out from under her. Dad came to the rescue, of course. He heard the kerfuffle, cried: "Hang on, Eleanor!" climbed over the wall and righted the steps. What a hero. Mrs Swanley was quite flustered. She had to have a cup of nettle tea for her nerves. "It was a horrible podgy beast," she quivered. "A strange sort of tan and black colour, it was. Never seen a rat quite like it before." I jumped up as soon as she said it. "That's no rat!" I shouted. "That's my guinea pig, Jupiter!" At which point, Mrs Swanley swooned.

While Dad was reviving her, I went on a GP hunt with Ginger. I stuffed a bit of Jupiter's straw under

Ginger's nose and instructed him to seek. He had a sneezing fit instead! And I couldn't find Jupiter anywhere. Gnash! But I know how he got out. We have an old-fashioned tumble-drier with a trunk that you have to dangle out of the window. Dad had taken it off to fix it but left one end trailing loose on the floor. My theory is that Jupiter crawled inside and was still in there when Dad connected it up again. I think the warm air blew him out. Like a guinea-pig cannon-ball! OK, OK, he might have crawled out. Have a look at the attachment I've

sent you. It's my map of Jupiter's escape route from cage to garden via tumble-drier. I did it with Dad's new painting package, PhotoPlay, which is ace. Oops, gotta go, I think I can smell Dad's sausages frazzling!

Annabelle Attenborough

PS Forgot to ask Dad why he's never said anything about you or your dad before. Soz. Does it matter?

QUESTIONNAIRE

Dear Annabelle,

I still don't know much about you, so could you please fill in the following details?

Hair Colour:
Eye Colour:
Height:
Build:
Best Subject at School:
Worst Subject at School:
Ambition:
Biggest Fear:
Talents:
Failings:

Thanks. My mock exams are pretty tedious. How are yours?

Best wishes,
Guy

MUM AND ME

Dear A,

You'll realize as soon as you get this: that was the hoax message, this is the real one. More about that later.

First, here's the photo you asked for. It's the Christmas before last – me, Mum and a turkey, taken by

Dad. (No, the turkey's the one on the table, before you ask. I'm the one on the left.) It's a great photo of Mum and I'm glad she put it in my album, but all I can think of when I look at it now is: She KNEW, by then. And I didn't. I didn't even guess. And when I look at myself there, all grinning and gormless, what I think is: What a senseless dork. How could he be sitting next to someone under a death sentence, and not even know it? Am I incredibly thick-skinned, or what? Anyway, it's obvious I'm not telepathic.

So – what do you think of my Mum? Is she how you expected? I like to think that she'll always be that age now – never old and grey and wrinkled.

Thanks for the picture of Jupiter's Great Escape – I hope you managed to round him up before he got into anything else. But where's the picture of you? I'm dying to see it. Are you telling the truth about the scanner?

Before we get on to Parents and their Strange Ways, let me tell you what happened to Dad yesterday. He had a sneezing accident! And no, I'm not making it up. It happened because the woman next door had come round to ask if I'd look after her cat next weekend, and Dad was all sneezy cos he'd just done the hoovering, and because we had a visitor he was trying to sneeze politely instead of giving a great big honk like he usually does. He must have strained his neck muscles or something, cos from then on he's been OOOhing and AAAARGhing around the house and can hardly back the car out of the drive cos it's agonizing to turn his head round. Whenever anyone asks how he did it, he can't say "In the gym" or "Playing rugger" or anything tough and manly – not when I'm there, anyway. "I did it sneezing" makes everyone laugh, so he's going short on sympathy. Not that he deserves sympathy after what I've found out. I discovered that he's really devious. And, even worse, I discovered that I'm really devious . . .

You know I said I deleted your messages? Well, that's not strictly true, because on our program trashed stuff is kept where you can get it back – it's only finally gone when you delete it from the recycling bin. Anyway, I decided to get your trashed messages back, just to remind myself how SNOTTY AND HORRIBLE you were at first. And guess what I found? Devious Dad must have thought he was really clever, finding out how to trash, but he doesn't realize that trashed stuff can still be called back. So there in the bin was a whole list of files DD thought he'd deleted.

What did I do? What would YOU do?

I read them. And –

(the hoax message, by the way, is to fool DD. He's getting curious about whether we're still mailing each other – why isn't there anything in the Out or

In boxes? "Is it secret?" he asked me. "Getting romantic or something?" So I humphed and told him not to be so mind-numbingly stupid. He's got a one-track mind – comes from a guilty conscience. So that hoax message is to keep him quiet. Honestly, it's so easy to fool my Dad, it's quite worrying.)

– what turns up is that Dad is having an e-mail FLIRTATION with some woman in Manchester called Sharon. Is that indecent, or what? My Mum's been dead just over six months, and already he's getting off with someone else. As far as I can gather they haven't actually met yet, so I suppose you couldn't technically say he's being unfaithful to Mum, but all the same it makes me feel sick. Wouldn't it make *you* feel sick? *Are* you feeling sick? I am. About to throw. Stand back from the screen.

What should I do? Should I confront him? I can tell he feels dead guilty about it, too. Over the Christmas holidays, he kept dropping hints that I ought to pick up my social life. "What's happened to that sweet girl Jess?" he kept saying. "Why don't you ask her out again? You ought to get out and enjoy yourself." Well, the fact is I don't *want* to enjoy myself. It's too *soon* to enjoy myself. And around Christmas I thought I'd never want to enjoy myself again. I put him off by saying I had my mocks coming up and course work to do and anyway I was having those few days in Yorkshire with Mark. But he keeps going on about Jess. What a nice girl she is, how pretty, how he wouldn't wait around if he was thirty years younger. It's only to make himself feel better about this ghastly Sharon.

Jess, by the way, is a girl in my form. I went out with her last year for six weeks and I was really keen on her, but well, you know what it's like at school. Everyone used to tease us rotten if we sat together in lessons or if we both came in late together. They'd call us Romeo and Juliet and make soppy slurpy kissing noises. And much worse things than that. In the end we both got so embarrassed that we stopped going out. And then, Mum got ill. Jess is going out with someone else now, only I can't be bothered to tell Dad. He'll think it's my fault for not trying.

Anyway, Parents and their Pasts. If you don't want to read this next bit, then don't, because I've found out something about your dad.

DD and I are on cool terms with each other at present, but tonight I asked him why he wanted me to e-mail you in the first place. He said, "Just an idea. If it doesn't work, forget it." So I told him how keen your Dad was for us to carry on, with the 50ps and all that. He gave me a funny look then, though it may have been cos his neck was still creaking. I said, "Why haven't I ever heard of Franklin? He's never been here, has he? I know he e-mails you about his accounts, but that's only boring stuff. I thought you were supposed to be friends?"

He'd got accounts sheets spread all over the table and was crunching numbers with his calculator, so it wasn't a very good time to ask. He went back to frowning at his figures, and muttered something about different ways of life. About your Dad being a tutor at Oxford University, which is a bit different from being a jobbing accountant.

"So what made you friends in the first place?" I asked. That's assuming they *were*. Cos the way it looks to me, my Dad doesn't like yours much.

"It was ages ago, I told you," he said. "We were students. The four of us shared a house, at York."

Well, I know my Mum and Dad met each other at university. So I said, "Four? You, Mum, Franklin and who else?" He muttered something about six and a half per cent under his breath and jabbed a few keys, then he said – wait for it!

"Um? What?" (Really on the ball, my Dad.) "Jane, of course. Jane and Franklin met at York too." Jane? I nearly bit my tongue in half. Then I asked him, what, the same Jane that took my christening photo? He gave me one of his withering looks and said that yes, Jane and your Dad were an item then, and could I please let him get on with his figures. But I wasn't going to give up, was I? Not on the trail of something hot. "Are you sure?" I said. And he snapped, "Yes! I'm perfectly sure," and carried on writing down numbers.

"But Annabelle's Mum's called M–" I started. And then he got really huffy and slammed his calculator down on the desk. A battery fell out and bounced off the table. While he was grovelling for it, he said, "Yes, I know, but back then it was Jane, OK? It was a steamy on-off thing. More off than on if I remember correctly." Then he got up rubbing his neck and said, "I'm trying to WORK, in case you hadn't noticed."

There. I TOLD you, didn't I? About your Dad's torrid affair? That locket you found is Jane's, I bet – that's why he doesn't want you asking awkward questions or telling your Mum.

Just then the phone rang and it was another one of Dad's clients, some everlasting tedious conversation about fixed-rate interest and personal pension plans. While he droned on, my mind was working triple-speed. If Jane shared the house, and she was at my christening, and you'd already been born in January, where does your Mum come in? Unless it was "on" with your Mum when it was "off" with steamy Jane?

So I tried asking Dad when he got off the phone. I said (all casual, of course), "Did Franklin have many 'items' at York?" He was looking for his diary and muttering to himself, but when I said that he straightened up and stared at me and I *heard* his neck creak this time. The way he looked was enough to shrivel me right up. If he'd glared for a nanosecond longer I'd have been a little smoking heap of charcoal on the carpet. And then he went: "Pete, for Guy's sake!" (He meant "Guy, for Pete's sake" – shows what a state he was getting into.) "What's Annabelle been saying?"

I told him, "Nothing". He flipped all the cushions on to the floor, and said, "Please go away, then. Can't you see I'm pushed for time? And now I've lost my bloody diary. I've got a meeting with a new client tomorrow and I'd like these figures to make sense if that's all right with you. Weren't you moaning about homework just now? Why don't you go and get on with it?" And he started looking in really stupid places like under the doormat and behind the clock. Eventually I found his diary, on the window-sill behind the curtains, where he'd put it while he was on the phone. Then he had the cheek to say, "A cup of coffee would go down well, if you're heading for the kitchen."

What I make of that is, your Dad had more luck with girls than mine did, and the poor old sod's still jealous. But if he's jealous of your Dad and hardly ever speaks to him, how did they ever get back together? And why do they want US to be friends?

Huh. Adults. And they think we're peculiar.

Annabelle, do you have other e-mail penpals besides me? I've only got one – Cal, who used to be at my school till he went back to Chicago. We e-mail each other about once a week, but it's pretty dull – mostly technical stuff, or he sends me weird things he's found on the Internet. I don't send/write to anyone else like this, but it strikes me that you're such a sociable person that you've probably got dozens of e-males. If you send them all such long messages as you've been sending me, I don't know how you find time for anything else! But then I bet you can type at high speed. I imagine you *talking* at high speed – am I right? Anyway, do you have any other male mailers? Just wondered.

Don't worry about Dad reading your messages. I always get in before him and I log on straight away. Just don't ever send me anything after ten p.m. I'm sure that's when he does his Furtive Flirting. And don't forget I want that picture as soon as your scanner's working!

My mock exams are nearly finished now – are you doing them too? Or were yours before Christmas?

Guy

IN ANSWER TO YOUR QUESTIONS

Dear STUFFY and PROUD,

If you think I was SNOTTY and HORRIBLE when we first wrote, you should go back and read some of YOURS, gorilla mush.

:P (that's Internet jargon for "I stick my tongue out and waggle it at you"). Right. Now that I have got that out of my hair and I am back to sweetness and light again (don't say it, Woodham), let us continue . . .

Thank you for your questionnaire. Here is my reply.

Hair Colour: changeable – at the moment vanilla with strawberry topping! Yum!!

Eye Colour: Dad says hazel; Mum says acorn; please ask the next squirrel you see.

Height: I am taller than Tracey Scudding, that's all you need to know.

Build: I BEG YOUR PARDON?! All my bits are in the right places in the right proportions, thank you very much! I have small ears (but they hear *everything*).

Best Subject at School: English, dummy. I am Ms Spence's star pupil.

Worst Subject at School: Geography. So what if penguins don't live at the North Pole? It's icy, isn't it? That's what counts. Trust you to be good at

Geog. Fancy orienteering over to Oxford and teaching me how to read a map? (Bat eyelid. Bat eyelid.)

Ambition: TO MEET YOU!!!! And to find Jupiter. And that locket. I had a poke round the cellar but it wasn't in there. What's Dad done with it? It's driving me barmy. I wonder if I dare go and look in the loft?

Biggest Fear: That there is no cat-flap in heaven. If I never see Hornbeam again I will die. (Erm, is that possible?)

Talents: Oh *purlease*. Where would you like me to begin? I can play the spoons, you know that. I can run the hundred metres in 19.8 seconds (if I saw Daniel Day-Lewis at that distance I would break the world record!!) I can stand on my head without showing my knickers. Do you want to know any more?

Failings: Come on, Guy! Don't ask such useless questions. I don't have failings. I have FILINGS – lots of them. I've just sharpened my pencil! Oh, all right. You'll only say I'm boasting if I don't answer properly. I suppose I could beat a crocodile in a snapping competition – but then I do have perfect teeth. Dad says I'm a bit aloof and uppity at times, especially when I meet new people. He says I get this from Mum. Huh. He'll be telling me next that Ginger is good at digging thanks to her. But I suppose he's right. I *was* a bit uppity with you at first, wasn't I? Dad calls it my "defence mechanism". I don't know what he means, though, really. Why would I want to defend myself against someone as nice as you? Dad says I do it because I get easily hurt and take things deep down. I suppose that's right, too. If you didn't write to me now it would be like losing Hornbeam all over again. That's pretty deep, isn't it? You will keep writing to me, won't you, Guy? Sorry. Sorry. SORRY! I'm getting all stupid and soppy and girly. I don't own you, do I? Change of subject: thanks for that smashing piccie of you and your mum. Wow, what a stunner. Your mum, I mean. Well, you do rather take after her in that department. I expect that Jess must be . . . Well, I don't know what I expect that Jess must be. Ignore that. I . . . oh no. I've got loads to tell you but Dad's shouting me down – grrr and dubble grrr'! We have to go to the doctor's now. Talk later. Promise.

Annabelle the aloof x

PS My mock exams are pretty tedious as well. Thanks.

PPS Who IS this Jane woman? I'm going to roast Dad's ears on the way to the doctor's. That should make him nice and steamy. Good with girls? My dad? MY dad?

PPPS You didn't ask when my birthday was. It's January 18th. I'm a Capricorn, a goat! (Don't know what the sign is for crocodiles, sorry.)

WHERE ARE YOU?

Dear Annabelle,

Are you ill? It *must* be you not your Dad, or why would you both go to the doctor? And you *promised* to talk later, but didn't! Is there something wrong? You're not seriously ill, are you? Please e-mail me back and tell me you're not. As soon as you get this.

Guy

PS Hey, was that an x you sent me? An actual x? If so, I'm dead chuffed. But perhaps it was only a typing mistake, or short for something – like X marks the spot, or Xtremely worried about going to the doctor.

There's one for you at the end of this, but beware – it might only be a typo, or a stray guinea-pig strolling over the keyboard. DON'T forget to let me know you're not seriously ill.

Guy x

URGENT

Dear Annabelle,

I'm getting seriously worried! Two messages from Cal but nothing from you. I can't believe you'd go *three* days without e-mailing me unless something was really wrong. Especially after, you know, what you said. You're not in hospital, are you? I haven't upset you, have I, with the x business or by joking about guinea-pigs?

PLEASE e-mail me! Another x (if you want it!),

Guy

CRASHERAMA!

AAAAAAAAAAAAAGGGGGGGGGGGGGHHHHHHH-HHHHH!

Guy, calm down That wasn't me being seriously ill. I can't yak over that sort of distance. I am just FUMING! Fuming! Fuming! FUMING!

I'm sorry it's taken ages to reply to your messages. Of course you didn't upset me, silly. Our komputer had krashed, so I couldn't mail you. Dad said it was because our server was down. I told him I didn't care if it was standing on its head and shaking all its wires, I had important G-mail to send! "It's no use being impatient," he said. But he was getting pretty raggy about it himself. Yesterday, he yelled down the phone at someone: "And what did your last SERVER die of, then?" (I think it was supposed to be some kind of joke.) Anyway, it took three whole days to come back up. THREE DAYS! I could have boiled 1,080 eggs in that time! This is a sort of in-joke, sorry. In Maths yesterday, Mr

Phiggins told us the perfect breakfast was an egg boiled for precisely four minutes. When Jamie Tarnock cheeked him and said the perfect breakfast was actually squashed tomatoes on peanut butter on toast, Mr Phiggins made Jamie calculate how many eggs, on average, are boiled in Oxford every day. Without a calculator, too.

Anyway, I am desperate to know if you have tried to send me anything else since your x followed by another x? Gosh, lucky me. That's an x for each cheek. (I expect that's where you were aiming them, wasn't it?) I asked Dad what happens to messages sent when servers have crashed and he just waved a hand and said, "Oh, it depends – if you're lucky they get stored in memory; if you're not, they disappear into the ether." Don't you hate it when dads swish you away like that? So I swished a punch at him and said, "You'll be telling me next that's where Jupiter's gone: the ether!" Bad move. That just made him think about the locket. He frowned and said did I want a lift to drama group tonight or not? Did I tell you I am auditioning for the role of Cleopatra for the end-of-term play? Me and Tracey Scudding are going for it. Scudding the Pudding! She hasn't got a hope. Ms Spence told Tracey that the Queen of the Nile was a woman of "enormous mystical elegance". Oh well, one out of three's not bad, I suppose (scratch, claw).
Actually, A & C is a very hard script. So hard that Ms Spence had to persuade the Head to let us do it.

"I told him I had the talent," she gushed. (I'm not sure if she was talking about herself or the drama group.) Carla Whitmore says she once heard Mr Bellingham call Ms Spence a "jumped-up, thwarted RSC director" after she refused to give up the gym to his T'ai Chi class one Thursday night. Who cares? Do you like drama? I bet you'd make a really good Caesar, actually. I can picture you as bold and brave and a leader of men. Try it. All you need is a tablecloth slung over your shoulder and a few leafy twigs around your head. Perhaps Mark could play Mark Antony? But then you'd be the one who gets stabbed in the back and Mark would get to x me into the bargain. You're right, Mark is quite good-looking, but I don't think I'd fancy a snog with him. He could audition for jaws with those teeth (don't you tell him!!). Now I come to think of it, *you* would make a good Mark Antony, but I think I will change the subject now . . .

It was sweet of you to be all concerned about me going to the doctors. You needn't have worried. It was only for a teency mole on my neck. I couldn't understand why Dad even bothered to make the appointment. I was brushing my hair before school one morning and he saw it and said, "Has that got bigger – the mole, I mean?" I just shrugged – and the next I knew we were off to Dr Keelan's. Dad insisted on coming in with me as well. Major embarrassment. Worse than having him around when I'm buying clothes. – I told him Laura Blackman's got so many moles you could practically do join the dots with them. But he wouldn't budge.

Anyway, Dr Keelan peeked at it with her torchy thing and said it seemed perfectly all right at the moment, but that she'd like to see it again in a few months' time.

"Why?" I said. She gave me a doctorly smile and said, "Sometimes if they grow they can be a health risk – and then they're best removed." "Will it leave a scar?" I asked. Dad tutted at that and rolled his eyes. "Thinking about the boys," he said to Doctor Keelan. Thinking about the *boys*? Hah! What a cheek! But I could see Dr Keelan looking at me, wondering. So I said "I've got an e-mail friend called Guy. You can't see moles over the Internet, *Dad*." Dr Keelan laughed and tapped something out on her own computer. 'The Practice has just got e-mail," she said. "I haven't quite mastered it yet. Did you meet your friend through a chat line or something?" I shook my head. "Dad introduced us." "Oh," said Dr Keelan, smiling again, "I didn't realize you were an e-mail expert, Dr King? Perhaps you could give me a few lessons sometime?"

For a second, everything went quiet. Then I looked up and couldn't *believe* what I was seeing. Dad and Dr Keelan were eyeing one another! She had this silly girly twinkle in her eye and he was giving it the Hornbeam with cream look. It made me really ratty. "He knows Guy's mum and dad," I snapped, kicking Dr Keelan's desk accidentally-on-purpose to get her attention. "They were all at university together – with Dad's steamy girl friend, Jane." Wow, that broke it up all right. Dad gave me such a look I thought his eyebrows would never untangle. And then I did a proper Brutus on him. I turned straight back to the doctor and said, 'Can I ask you about my periods, now?' Dad went GREEN from top to bottom. Serves him right for being such a flirt.

I know how you must feel about your dad, now. It must have been horrible, finding out about Sharon. And of course you were right to read his e-mails. They'd read ours if they got the chance. At first I was going to write and say that perhaps you were being a bit harsh on your dad. I mean, you don't *know* that Sharon's ghastly, do you? Or do you? Did you find any decent goss on her in the trash? I was going to say something really kind, like dads are only people and they can get lonely,too. But that was before I knew THE TRUTH ABOUT JANE.

In the car, on the way home, me and Dad didn't speak for ages. But I just couldn't stop myself looking at him. I've only ever thought of him as "Dad" before; I've never imagined him as anything fanciable. Mrs Swanley thinks he's wonderful, though. And now I come to think of it there's this woman in the bread shop who's always cracking jokes about "which way would he like it sliced?" and "would he like a nice sticky bun with it, too?"

Yuk, she really *is* ghastly. Anyway, back to the car.

Eventually he noticed me looking, and cracked. "Annabelle," he said, "if I've something hanging out of my nose, please say." I crossed my arms and sniffed. "She fancied you, that Dr Keelan." He tutted loudly and shook his head. "You've been doing too much drama group," he muttered. Oh, ha ha.

We turned a corner in silence. Then, amazingly, he started on this: "And what was all that about 'Jane', in there? What's Guy been saying? I'm really beginning to rue the day I suggested this little e-mail alliance." I kicked out a leg. "Why did you then?" He went quiet and batted his indicator on. "I told you, I thought you might be good for one another." He looked across and I turned my face away. "All right," he sighed. "If you really must know, Guy's dad and I go back a long way–" "York," I cut in, "about two hundred miles." He snatched at the gear stick and thrust it forward. "If you're going to act smart I'll let you stew." I hurred on my nails, praying he'd go on. Fortunately, he did.

"Yes, I met Guy's dad at York. For three years we shared a house together. We were good friends then, and . . . we are again now. And before you ask – yes, I knew Guy's mother as well. She was one of the other people in the house." At this point, I risked an interruption. "Was JANE in the house as well?" That made him grind his teeth. You could almost *hear* him gnashing up the guilt. "Yes," he confessed, looking right for traffic. “There was me and Tom Woodham – Guy’s dad, of course; Mary, who later became Tom’s wife; and my . . . girlfriend, Jane.” That was a painful moment. When he said “Jane” he had the nerve to *smirk*. But not for long.

“You had an affair with her, didn’t you?” I accused him. Do you know what he did? He started to laugh! ”You’re allowed to have affairs with your girl-friend,” he said.But I wouldn’t let it go. I hotched round in my seat and shouted: “That’s her locket I found, isn’t it?” He pinched his lips and put his shoulders back “Annabelle,” he said. “forget you ever saw that locket. I don’t want you searching for it or telling anyone about it. Not Guy. Not Ms Spence–” “Not Mum?” I shouted. “Tough, she already KNOWS.” I bounced around again and faced the door. He let out a whopping dad-sized sigh.

By now, I was getting a little bit sniffy. All sorts of things were running through my mind – about you, your mum, my mum far away in Egg-whipped. “You still love Jane, don’t you?” I blubbed, wanting him to say, “Of course not, petal. I will only ever love your bone-digging mum.” But he didn’t. He pulled on to our drive, switched the engine off and said, “Part of me will always be in love with Jane.” And then I flipped – and made a real blooper.

Ohhh Guy, I’m not sure I should be telling you this. I have got the most awful confession to make. I know I could easily have kept it a secret. That's the thing about e-mail, isn't it? You don't have to worry about saying the wrong thing. But I know I won't sleep if I don't tell the truth. I'm just worried if I do that you might not ever want to write to me again. Please don't say I was horrible or anything. I don't know how it happened, it just . . . did. When Dad said he'd always be in love with Jane, I tugged against my seatbelt and howled right at him "Well I hate her! I hate her! I HATE that JESS!"

There. It's out. I meant to say Jane and I didn't, I said Jess. "Jess?" said Dad. "Who on earth is . . .?" But that was as far as it got. I jumped out, slammed the door and ran to my room. I'm sorry, it's no good pretending, is it? I expect you've guessed. I was really jealous.

And now I don't think I can say any more until I know what you think of me.

Sorry.
A
x (if you want it)
x anyway (if you don't)

HAPPY BIRTHDAY TO YOU...
HAPPY BIRTHDAY TO YOU...
HAPPY BIRTHDAY TO YOU...

For my favourite e-mail pal.
Because you're an
A stonishingly
N ice
N eurotic
A musing
B ewildering
E nergetic
L oquacious
L ovable
E xtrovert

BIRTHDAY GIRL IN HEAVEN!

Dear Guy,

This might seem a very strange message. It's sort of in two parts. I have just popped into the Internet Post Office and picked up your WONDERFUL birthday card.I have also noticed the date it was sent: exactly one day before my last letter to you. I think our messages have sort of . . . crossed in the ether.

If, by now, you have read my last letter to you and you do not wish to know me any more, I fully understand. I was very silly going on about Jess and I apologize. Please put it down to another phase of immaturity I am probably going through. So I will end part one by saying thank you for my card. It was absolutely brilliant. I really mean that. I am lucky to have had a friend like you.

Yours,
Annabelle King

If, on the other hand, you have read my message and you don't mind the things I said and you are willing to carry on writing to a neurotic extrovert (excuse me?) like me, you won't mind this . . .

YES! Oh wow! What a GREAT GUY you are! I don't know what to say! I am STUMPED. I am 'STONISHED. I am all out of GUSH! Can you believe it? Me? Lovable Loquacious – with nothing to say? Hang on, something is trickling through . . .

my nimmy nammy nommy (don't worry, that's just my bewildering brain at work). Dear Woodham, you are a

G orgeous
U nbelievable
Y UNK!

Sorry, that was the closest I could get to hunk! Yee! That is the BEST birthday card I have EVER had. You are SO CLEVER! How did you do it? Singing chipmunks? That's you and Mark speeded up, isn't it? And where did you find that video clip of Rodeo Ronson? I've never seen that before. He looks a bit silly in that cowboy hat and those dungarees, doesn't he? I think I am going off Rodeo Ronson, but I am definitely not going off you. Oops.

Oh, Guy. I am so happy; even if you ARE mad at me for being a silly jealous A. I will cherish this card for ever and ever – and its xxx. That's five now, you know. Gosh, I won't know what to do with –

Hhh Guy, you'll never guess what's happened? Dad just popped his head round the door to see what all the paddling of feet was about. So I played your birthday card for him. He stood there, behind me, smiling over my shoulder and all the time I had no idea what he had in his arms. I wouldn't mind, but I actually looked at him TWICE! It was only when he muttered, "Hmm, he thinks you're lovable, does he?" that I turned right around. And then I saw it. "Happy birthday," Dad said. "I hope it's what you want."

Oh Guy, he's really sweet. His name is Rocket. He is silver grey with some black in his tail – and he's just gone and peed in my lap!

Please write soon
Wet of Oxford

PLOT THICKENS IN SEVERAL DIRECTIONS

Dear Astonishingly Nice, etc. (Had trouble with loquacious. Had to use the dictionary for that one. But it fits!) Glad you liked my card. Took me hours, specially finding the bit of Rodeo Ronson on the Internet and working out how to copy it. I'm glad you're going off him, cos I think he's a total nerd.

I'll go with the second of your two messages, if you don't mind. You're not getting rid of me that easily.

So – who is Rocket the pee-er? Cat, guinea-pig, Egyptian ocelot? And apart from being peed on, I hope you had a great birthday. You're a bit older than me – does that matter? I won't be sixteen till August. That means I'm the youngest in my year, but at least I always have my birthday in the summer holidays.

Anyway, I'm glad it was nothing serious at the doctor's. What's with our Dads, doing all this flirting with Doctors and Sharons? Mid-life crisis? And even your Mum by the sound of it – she hasn't eloped with an Ancient Egyptian, has she? Is she getting her own back on your Dad for having an everlasting Thing about Steamy Jane? When's she coming home? And is there any more progress with the Mystery of the Floorboards?

Have you had your mock results back yet? I did OK in all mine, except the French oral.

Good luck with your audition for Cleopatra. I'd be useless in a play, but I bet you'll be brilliant. And I hope you get a yunky Mark Antony, not Mark-my-sometimes-friend, who's staying here this week (watching something trashy downstairs, not reading this over my shoulder). More about him in a minute. How can you find time for such a big play in your GCSE year? Aren't you bogged down with course work deadlines and panic? Or are you so brilliant that you can do it all *and* play Cleo?

Oh, and back at the doctor's – Dr King! That threw me for a minute till I worked out that your Dad's not a medical doctor, he's the other kind, a Professor or whatnot. He must be incredibly brainy – no wonder my Dad's got a mega-sized Dr Franklin King inferiority complex.

You know what he said, about different ways of life? Well, that's started to bother me a bit. Your Dad being a real Dr, and living in a big house in Oxford and everything. I bet your parents have brilliantly clever friends and they come to your brilliantly clever parties and say brilliantly clever things to each other. I'm just ordinary, you've got to realize. Doesn't Dr Franklinstein know dozens of sons of rocket scientists or nuclear physicists who've got e-mail? We live in an ordinary semi and my Dad's an accountant and my Mum worked in a school library. I'm nothing special. That's not saying I'm thick or a yob or anything, cos I'm not, but remember I'm just an Ordinary Guy.

An Ordinary Guy with a Dad problem. It's several degrees sub-zero round here and unlikely to thaw. Dad remarked, all casual, when we were having our cornflakes the other morning: "I'm going to be away for a couple of days. Going to our Manchester office to sort out a problem. You can have Mark to stay if you like." Well, you'll probably think this was really devious, but this is what I did. Mark came round after school and I got him to phone my Dad's office, pretending to be a sales rep or something, and ask for the phone number of the Manchester office. Guess what? They haven't GOT a Manchester office! He's going to see Sharon, that's where he's going.

The cheat. The liar. How could he?

WHAT SHOULD I DO? Should I confront him with it when he gets back? Always supposing he does come back. What if he doesn't? I'm too young to be a householder.

Anyway, about Mark. Here's why we're not best mates just now, though we're lumbered with each other for a whole week. We went walking on Offa's Dyke on Saturday (training for our Major Expedition), and while we were up in the woods a grey squirrel ran out and sat on the path in front of us. I must have been feeling a bit daft and happy for once, cos I said: "Hey, Mr Squirrel, what colour are Annabelle's eyes? Hazel or acorn?"

Of course Mark wanted to know who Annabelle was, so I said my e-mail friend. He said: "That's great, you meeting someone new, cos now you won't mind so much." "Mind what so much?" I demanded. "That I'm going out with Jess now," he said, all casual. (I know never to trust people when they go All Casual.)

Well! I didn't know whether to explode or go silent and huffy. I went silent and huffy. I'd heard that Jess was going out with someone from another school (Mark goes to the posh grammar school – I go to the comprehensive. That doesn't mean he's cleverer than me, cos he's as thick as a very thick plank sometimes) but I'd never have dreamed it was Mark. My mate, or I thought he was. And I don't know whether I'm more annoyed with him or with Jess. He said, "Well, you dumped her, didn't you?" I tried to say it wasn't really like that, but he wouldn't believe me. Then, just now, he asked if I'd mind if he phoned her. Mark isn't the most sensitive person, as you're probably starting to think. If you're jealous of Jess (I can't really believe you were) it can be because she's going out with Mark now. I was so narked that I nearly told him what you said about Jaws. Or even that you thought I looked nicer than him. But I knew what he'd say back, so I didn't.

Then, when I'd stopped huffing (still on Offa's Dyke, or Huffa's Dyke as it should have been called that day) he asked me what you were like. I started to tell him . . . and then he went, "But how do you know?"

"How do I know what?" I said, still miffed.

And he said, "How do you know she's who she says she is? You think you're writing to a sixteen-year-old girl, but for all you know she might be a . . . well, say, a forty-three-year-old bloke sitting at a computer somewhere, pretending to be Annabelle. You hear of things like that on Internet chat lines."

So I said, "That's rubbish. Anyway, our parents know each other." "But have you seen a photo of her?" he asked. And I had to say no, I haven't.

(Though even if I had, that wouldn't prove it was really you. He's got me all neurotic and suspicious now.) BUT PLEASE SEND ME ONE ANYWAY!

Well – you asked what I think of you. I can't believe the way you've changed from the beginning. I didn't like you at all – I thought you were big-headed and self-centred and lots of other things. But now – I really don't know what I think. Specially cos of not having your picture. What I can truthfully say is that you're clever and funny and not like anyone else I've met. And I go up to my computer every day as soon as I come home. And I'm really disappointed if there isn't a message from you.

Guy

PS I told a lie just now. I hope you DON'T get a yunky Mark Antony.

HOSTAGE IN OWN HOME, THANK YOU VERY MUCH!

Dear Guy,

As you have probably gathered from the subject title, this message is not from Annabelle. It is from Franklin, Annabelle's FATHER. Hello. I'm sorry, I don't mean to sound as if I'm shouting or angry when I capitalize like that. That was an instruction from my darling daughter, who is standing beside me holding me at "claw point". Stay with me. All will become clear in a moment.

You may be wondering why you are getting a message from me at all, especially as I have ESSAYS to mark and an important TUTORIAL to prepare for tomorrow! Yes, thank you, Annabelle. She has just waved a cat's paw close to my face and warned me to get on with it. This is the sort of girl you are writing to, Guy: one who holds her father hostage over the computer with the threat of "several deep scratches" if he doesn't do as he's told. Hang on –

I am instructed to explain to you that Rocket is not a guinea pig, *stupid* (her words, not mine; also her emphasis), he is a cat – a kitten to be precise. Oh Lord – said kitten has now just struggled out of her arms and rocketed under the wardrobe. While she struggles to retrieve it, I would like to take this opportunity to point out to you and my tenacious little firebrand of a daughter that they said nothing at the RSPCA about "this cat may be used as a weapon against you". Ah, she's back. Good Lord, that last line actually made her smile. It won't if I return the furry little so and so to the shelter whence it came.

Oh dear, that last remark seems to have made her pout again. I am now instructed to "do the business". Are you ready?

This is the business: Annabelle is not very happy with you right now. She is refusing to speak to you for "questioning her integrity". Actually, she used the word "honesty" there, but I felt integrity was the word she was after once she had explained the nature of the problem. This is one of the reasons she's top of the class in English: her beloved father has taught her all she knows – and this is how she repays him!

All right! All right! She is now saying that Rocket is

getting very twitchy and she cannot guarantee he will stay calm much longer. Apparently, if I want to "listen to my boring old Beethoven with both ears tonight" I am to get on with my/her objective and confirm to you that:

a) our scanner is DEFINITELY broken.

b) you are a toad for not believing her (twice) – that's wbo ("with bells on") by the way.

c) Mark (whoever he is) is an even bigger toad, and – a what? Oh, a slimy one at that.

d) If you point your browser at http://www.weaver-parkschool.photofile.htm you might see something you like. I have no idea what this something is but madam says, somewhat cryptically, "It's a game of elimination; pick the wrong one at your peril". Guy, I wish you luck. And believe me, I know what you're feeling right now. Hang on –

Sorry, I am to stop being "spontaneous" (I think she means autonomous, actually) and inform you there is an e).

e) please read b) again.

Finally, though Lord knows how, I am to reassure you that it really is Annabelle's father writing this, and that all Annabelle's messages are "properly" from her. [Tch! No wonder Jenny Spence says Annabelle's grammar needs attention.] Oh, now I am accused of philandering for giving "Ms" Spence a Christian name!

So, how do I make you believe that this is me? I suppose by telling you something my petulant petal could not be expected to know, but that your father (Tom) will understand – yes?

Yes. I've got the go-ahead. OK. Ask your dad if he remembers the pancake incident at Caverner Road. If he can't tell you the entire story, you know this is a fake. I'm afraid I can't think of a better way to prove to you that Annabelle's messages are genuinely from her. But if tomorrow's headlines go something like: "OXFORD DON SAVAGED BY MAD KITTEN" and you're continuing to get messages after that, you will at least be able to eliminate me from your list of suspects.

I think this concludes our contact. Lovely to talk to you. Do you mind if I say I'm sorry about your mum? She was a wonderful lady and a true friend. If you grow up to be anything like her you will be a fine young man.

Yours, unscathed (thank goodness),
Franklin Murrayfield King

Hang on, there's a PS. She says . . . PS You must eliminate two (successfully) by midnight tonight or you will never hear from her again.

Hang on – there's more . . . PPS That's a promise.

Annabelle, please, I have work to do! (Sorry Guy, she's thinking. That was a very clever birthday card, by the way.) Ah, at last . . . PPPS If it comes down to her and Tracey Scudding and you get the wrong one she will not answer for the consequences. Goodbye.

And from me, FMK:)

E-MAILER COMMITS HARA-KIRI

Dear Firebrand,

HANG ON! This isn't fair. I would like to air the following grievances:

1. It was MARK who suggested you weren't real, not me. Any further amphibian insults should be directed at him. Actually, I like toads. But not Mark.

2. At least I gave you a fifty-fifty chance of guessing which was me! Your odds are unfairly stacked against me. I've looked up your school web site and you must mean the photo of the Year Nine netball team, unless you're the caretaker planting a tree or the grinning person collecting the Industry award or the girl in the Library who's deeply engrossed in a deeply unengrossing-looking book.(No, she must be Sixth Form. Or perhaps a very young teacher).So, I'll assume you mean the netball team and you want me to work out which is you.

NO. I am not playing Russian Netball Roulette, thank you. (Question: Is your school so desperate for morale-boosting pictures that it has to use netball pictures from two years ago?) Here are my two and only guesses, so if I don't hear from you again I'll know I'm wrong on one or both counts.

You are NOT the one on the left front who looks innocent and angelic. You ARE (wait – just checking I've got my doctor's phone number handy) the one on the far right with the cheeky grin and the legs. PLEASE don't tell me that's Tracey Scudding . . .

Please tell your Dad, thanks for his message, especially what he said about Mum. He sounds just like you, sort of Annabelle on overdrive, but I *do* believe it was really him. I'll check out the pancake story when Dad comes home, if we're on speaking terms.

Your soon-to-be-ex-friend,
Guy Alexander Woodham

PS Why does your Dad use his middle name? Has he got a short-surname inferiority complex?

TOAD OUT OF A HOLE

Guy Alexander Woodham, you are not just an ex-toad, you are a SPAWNY ex-toad and probably covered in jam into the bargain. You must have been kissed by a very magical princess in your time in a pond, that's all I can say. You are the sort of person my mum would say could stick their hand in a bucket of sludge and pull out a peanut. No, *I* don't know what it means, either. It's just something she says, OK?

I'm sorry, I am being a bit raggy. I can't help it. I'll tell you why in a minute. But before I do, please be informed that one lucky guess does not get you entirely off the hook. For instance, what do you mean by "the legs"? What's wrong with my legs? There are two of them, aren't there? And yes, they go right up to my armpits. I s'pose you think they're too skinny, don't you? Well, I have grown a bit since Year Nine, silly. And how should I know why they want to use a picture from two years ago? They probably thought it was a good one of *her*, Scudding (Wing Attack). Spit! If you saw that picture now you would probably go: "Phwoarr, catwalk legs!" and I don't mean bandy and furry, either. Just watch it, OK? You are still on probation – and in case you're wondering, I didn't have to ask Franklinstein D Murrayfield Roosevelt for that word either. I thought of it all by myself.

Huh.

And if you think I've got a cheeky grin you should see my SCOWL. If you look out of your bedroom window RIGHT NOW you will probably see what looks like a thunder cloud coming your way. It is not. It is me, beaming my DARK MOOD towards you. I am doing this because I have been BETRAYED.

Twice. In a day.

I am not a very happy or funny bunny right now.

1. This morning, in English, Ms Spence said this: "Pay attention, class. For the next few weeks we're going to tackle something fresh and exciting!" As she turned away to clean the board, Gina Potterton (Goal Shooter) passed me a note. "Dewthorpe's underpants, not!" it said. I snickered and passed the note to Laura (Goal Defence). Just then, Kevin Dewthorpe looked over his shoulder and Laura creased. She made a sound like a sneezing donkey. That set me off, too, of course. Straight away Ms Spence said, "Laura Blackman. Annabelle King. Stand up, please." To make things worse, Sarah Hopkins (Wing Defence; the "angelic-looking" one) had the note by now. Ms Spence saw her with it and held out her hand. Sarah had to take the note to the front. "Hmm," went Ms Spence, "Gina Potterton's hand if I'm not mistaken." She glared across the back row. Gina blushed and got to her feet. Ms Spence scrunched the note up into a ball. "Well," she said, "I appear to have captured half the netball team. Let's hope you're all as adept at POETRY as you are at . . ." She lobbed the note across her desk and straight into the bin, "scoring goals." The rest of the class cheered and applauded. I just wanted to shrivel. "Poetry?" I wailed. "Oh yes," said Ms Spence. "Terribly evocative means of self-expression, Annabelle. And you four girls will be the first to experience the thrill and delight of verse construction as you'll all be

staying in at break finding twenty words that rhyme with underpants . . . The class roared with laughter. (There, that proves that poetry is pants.) "But Ms *Spence*," I groaned. "Poetry's *horrible*." Ms Spence just grinned and waved a few books. "You won't think that by the time you've studied the experts, Annabelle. In a few weeks' time I guarantee the stanzas will be positively *gushing* out of you . . ."

Hmph. I expect you would like to know the name of the first "expert" who is going to make me "gush"? Guy Woodham, if I hear so much as a titter in your next message you are straight back in the pond, OK? Cue drum roll as I open the envelope. AND THE FIRST EXPERT IS . . .

Wilfred Owen.

Remember, my little ears are better than radar. They are sweeping the Welsh border even as I write.

2. Scudding the Pudding has got the part of Cleo. I am to be her first maid, Charmian. I do not want to discuss this further. It is late at night. I am going to bed. I will send this in the morning if I have not been over-whelmed by gloom in my sleep.

Goodnight.

Hello. It is morning. Rocket says, "Yeep". I have just read through what I wrote last night and it sounds horrible. But what are friends for if you can't have a moan at them sometimes? I promise I will try to be happier today. BEAM! That was my cheeky grin at work. I think it's time we had an update, don't you?

First, Dad says he doesn't know anyone called Sharon. I asked him while we were washing up last night. "I think she lives in Manchester," I said. He waggled his doofer at a greasy plate. "Sorry, never heard of her. I knew a Karen there once, if that's any help?" I whacked him with a tea-towel. I don't THINK he was fibbing, but you never know with dads. I could torture him a bit, if you like? And, Guy, you MUSTN'T confront your dad about Sharon. If you do, he'll know you've read his e-mails, won't he? I think you should wait and see what happens – and keep on checking the trash. If you send me some of the messages you found I could read them and give you my expert sleuthing opinion. Perhaps he isn't off to see Sharon at all? Perhaps Sharon is a red herring or something? Have you ever seen a red herring? Dad likes fish and it's my turn to cook.

Exams are boring. I would rather not talk about them. My mock results were OK. I did quite well in English and Music, thank you.

Our server going sprongle. I meant to say this in my KRASHERAMA message but forgot. When our server was down and you were worried about me, why didn't you just give me a ring? Your dad must have our number. I wouldn't have minded. I think it would be nice to have a proper chat, don't you? Only if you wanted to. I'm not being pushy. It's just . . . don't you think it's funny that we say so much but neither of us knows what we actually sound like? Have you got an accent? You have *got* to tell me. I love accents. My mum says I talk like the Queen's favourite dog. I think she means posh – with the occasional yap (huh). It's my gran's fault for sending me to elocution lessons when I was young. I think Dad wishes it was electrocution lessons sometimes. I don't mean that. He loves me, really. Nice, sweet Daddy who's still giving me an extra two quid every week. Anyway, our number is 01865 11207. Call me any time you like, OK?

Names. My dad only uses his full name for "official correspondence". Congratulations, you are now official. The Murrayfield bit is because Dad was almost born during a Scotland vs England rugby match at Scotland's national stadium: Murrayfield. Gran was barely two weeks from popping but insisted on going to see the match. Legend has it (yawn) that if England won they would achieve something called the Grand Slam and win the Five Nations tournament. (Rugby; it's worse than football, I think.) Anyway, during the second half someone kicked the funny-shaped ball over the funny-shaped posts and the ball sailed into the crowd. Gran was so excited she leapt up to catch it and promptly went into labour. When my grandad asked her what was wrong she said she was about to perform the best "touch-down" of the day and could he arrange an ambulance, please? She had to be carried onto the pitch. Imagine that? Bursting with a baby and being surrounded by a load of muddy gorillas (no offence) in shorts.

Gran loved it. She got the autograph of someone called a "fly half" and even made the England captain blush when she pointed to her tummy and said, "It were a right rum scrum that started this off!" As they carted her away on a stretcher, the crowd cheered and sang, *Swing Low, Sweet Chariot*. Gran says it was the happiest moment of her life. When she found out later that England had won she called Dad "Murrayfield" so she'd never forget the day. Not much fear of that. Dad tells the story to anyone who'll listen. He always claims she was born on the pitch. I believed him for years until one day Mum had his horoscope done and she wrote his time of birth at ten minutes to midnight. Somehow, I don't think the game went on *that* long. If he ever starts to spout this fib at you, all you have to do is snigger and say, "Nice TRY, Franklin" and that shuts him up instantly. I don't know where the Franklin bit comes from. A film, I think. My middle name is Hermione by the way – pronounced Her-my-oh-knee not Her-me-own, please, or it's the pond again for you. Next.

I just re-read this:

> You know what he said, about different ways of
>life? Well, that's started to bother me a bit. Your
>Dad being a real Dr, and living in a big house in
>Oxford and everything. I bet your parents have
>brilliantly clever friends and they come to your
>brilliantly clever parties and say brilliantly clever
>things to each other. That's not saying I'm thick
>or a yob or anything, cos I'm not, but remember
>I'm just an Ordinary Guy.

Brilliantly clever parties? Come off it, Guy. The last time we had anything like a party was when we had our kitchen extended and the builders let me play cards with them. Tea and sweaty ham sandwiches we had. Thrilling. Dad hates parties. Books, Beethoven and solitude is what he likes – and rugby, of course. I saw Dad "dancing" at a wedding reception once. He looked like he was miming apple-picking. It was so embarrassing. I had to hide in the loos. I suppose we have got a fairly big house, but it's so full of books you can hardly see the walls. Your mum would have loved it. It's just like a library. I keep thinking we should have some *Shush!* signs up or one of those things that bleeps if you walk out without having a book stamped. You'd like my mum. She's quite good fun. She took me ten-pin bowling, once. And she often comes swimming with me and Laura. She listens to the radio a lot. Drama, mostly, and something called *The Archers.* I once asked her what she thought of Pineapple Pieces and she said they gave her indigestion. I didn't bother to explain they were top of the charts; she'd have probably asked, "At which supermarket, A?"

Funnily enough, Laura keeps nagging me to have a party. In break yesterday we started a list of top invitations. It was a bit like choosing sides for netball. "Spice Girls!" she cried. "Old news," I tutted. 'What about . . . Daniel Day-Lewis?" She rolled her eyes to the ceiling. "Zimmer frame," she scoffed. "OK, Prince William," I said. She drummed her fingers. "Probably off skiing. Let's ask David Beckham!" I aimed a finger down my throat. "Married a Spice Girl."

Laura gave an understanding nod. "Well," she said coyly, "we could always invite your e-mail pal. The one you never TALK about." I just smirked and hurred on my nails. "I think he's up a mountain this weekend,"I simpered. "Mountain?" she went. "Boring or what?" "What," I said. "Actually, he's not a bit boring. He's thoughtful and caring and quite funny at times. Not a bit like the posers we get round here." "What's his name?" she badgered. (She's dying to know.) "Not telling you," I sniffed. "Is he rich?" she pressed (it's Laura's ambition to marry a prince – if she ever grows up). I shook my head "Nope," I said. "He's just an ordinary . . . Guy," (I know, I'm a horrible tease,) "and he's absolutely *brilliant*."

There, Bet that made your head swell, Woodham. Anyway, to shut Laura up I promised I'd show her your birthday card. You don't mind if I show you off a little bit, do you? You might think you're ordinary; I think you're special. Oops. Blush, blush. Time to move along . . .

Animal update. Jupiter is still at large in the garden. We think he's alive because I keep finding pooh pellets here and there and under Dad's feet. The garden is big, like the house, and there is lots for a hungry Jupiter to eat. Dad says we should be more concerned about the weather than Jupiter getting totally lost. He says that guinea pigs don't like the cold and that Jupiter will probably come in when it gets a bit nippier. Last night, I tried to persuade Dad to put a guinea-pig flap in the back door, just in case J has been knocking at night. "Don't be silly," he said. 'Well, Hornbeam used one," I sulked. "He was a cat," said Dad. "Agile and clever. He didn't have the brain of a roly-poly pudding. If Jupiter can't eat it, sleep in it or pooh on it, it's meaningless to him." Which I thought was a little bit *piggist*, actually.

Ginger is just Ginger. He flops around the house staying out of Rocket's way. Yesterday, Rocket was swinging off his tail! Ginger only got mad when Rocket jumped on his back and dug his claws in a bit too hard. Rocket likes exploring, did I tell you that? He has been in the cellar (twice), the airing cupboard (four times) and yesterday the boot of the car (he picked a fight with an oily rag and had to be shampooed; he didn't like that). He is desperate to get in the garden too (he sits in the kitchen window a lot, getting spiked by the cactus plants), but I daren't let him out in case he wanders off and explores the road. He eats everything in sight. Last week he chewed a hole in Dad's best jumper. He has also had my French homework and some scrambled egg I slopped on the floor. He beats Ginger to food drops every time. I love him. He's fun. I still miss Hornbeam, of course. But Rocket is . . . Rocket. A bit barmy (like me!).

Mum. I had a postcard yesterday! It was a picture of some ancient Egg-whipped ornaments in a museum in Cairo. That set me off about the locket of course. Things have gone a bit quiet since the day that Mum rang up and she and Dad had their big locket barney. I'm not allowed to talk about it, even now. And I still haven't found the pesky thing. I've looked everywhere, Guy. I'm beginning to wonder if Dad hasn't melted it down and made it into Rocket's bell. Rocket's locket! Well, maybe not. He could hardly carry a lump like that around.

But I'm sure that locket is in the house somewhere. Tell you why. At the weekend, Dad went out and bought something called mortise bolts for the back door. When I asked him what they were for he said it was something to do with "insurance requirements".

He also bought something called a PM device which he stuck up in a corner of the hall, pointing at the front door. It has an infra-red beam and when you cross it it sets off a horrible shrieking alarm. That didn't last long.

Once Rocket found out how to set it off (eight times one night) Dad took it straight down again. He seems very anxious for Mum to come home, and I don't think it's much to do with pining for her, either. Anyway, his wish is going to be granted. Mum said in her card, "Missing you lots, A Slight c.o.p." (that's Mum-speak for "change of plan"). "Home sooner than expected. Get hoover out." (Cheek. I am the tidiest person I know! Are you?) Then she put, "Do as F says, there's a good girl. Happy b'day. See you soon. Love, Mum." Weird. She *never* puts "Do as Dad says". Why? What for? It's almost as if she was worried about something. I'm keeping up with my schoolwork and everything. Must be all that sand she eats. Or maybe she's feeling guilty about her Arab boyfriend . . .

Which reminds me, I have some things to say about Mark – and Jess. I think Mark *is* a toad – but only for not telling you sooner about Jess. Perhaps he fancied her all along while you were going out with her and was waiting to pounce if you ever did split, which you did, of course . . . sort of. I say "sort of" because I don't think you've split quite properly from her. Not where it matters.

Inside. In your heart. You said you went all silent and huffy when Mark said he was going out with her now. I think that means that part of you still loves her, doesn't it? just like part of my dad still loves Jane. I am going to assume that this is why you didn't send an x with your last two letters: that you still love Jess and think you are two-timing her. If you are going to try and win her back from Mark then I will cross my fingers for you, as a true friend should. I do want to be your friend, Guy Woodham – even if you don't do as you're told sometimes. I would be disappointed if my mail box was empty now, too. You asked me once if I had other e-mail friends. The answer is no. I have never had a proper boyfriend either but . . . hang on, there is someone at the door.

Guy, it's the police! Two of them. In suits. They wanted to know if they could speak to Dad. I told them he'd gone into town – which is a fib. He's next door, having coffee at Mrs Swanley's. They didn't seem to believe me either when I told them Mum was camped up the Nile. They have gone away now. I am going next door. Guy, *the police*. What's going on?

Gotta run, soz.
A (x)

1 OF 5: PICK-YOUR-OWN

Dear You-with-the-Legs,

Thanks for your letter, which has sent my head into overdrive – pretty amazing really, as it was definitely in underdrive after RE this afternoon. But, to get straight down to the serious business: have you found out about the police yet? Is it important or were they just coming to bring Jupiter back, after a tip-off from the local guinea-pig warden? (I don't mean that wouldn't be important, before you attack me. I mean was it something *criminal*?) But are you sure they were police, as they were in suits? Did they show you their ID cards? I hope you checked. Sorry, I don't mean to sound like your Dad or your form-teacher, but you have to be careful.

Here are your choices. If it's all been sorted out and you're in the mood for a New Mystery Development, progress to e-mail No. 2.

For More About Wilfred, go to No.3.

If you're in the mood for hearing more about Jess, progress to No. 4.

And for When Guy Wanted to Sink Through the Floor, go to No. 5.

Do Not Pass Go. Do Not Collect Two Hundred Pounds. This is Woodham's Pick-Your-Own Mail Service.

PS Was it Inspector Morse who came round? If so, you needn't worry. He never solves anything. He just waits till all the suspects have killed each other.

2 OF 5: WHAT'S *SHE* DOING OUT THERE?

Baffling development. Dad usually snatches up the post the moment it pokes though the letter-box, but while he's in Manchester I've been getting to it first. Guess what plopped on to our doormat yesterday? A postcard from JANE (she who has a little piece of your Dad's heart), that's what. Or at least I assume its the same Jane! If so, did you know she's out in Egypt? Coincidence, or does she know your Mum? The card comes from Luxor and there's a picture of a ram-headed sphinx from Karnak (well, that's what it says on the back. I bet an Egg-whip-perologist's daughter like you can recognize a ram-headed sphinx at ten paces.) Her writing's pretty awful but I think this is what she says: "Dearest Tom, This smug sheep reminded me of you, so I couldn't resist. MM would have liked it, wouldn't she? I gather A and G have taken off? I'm finishing here a bit earlier than expected, so home soon. Expect a phone call! It's time we met up again, Jane." And xxv (that's x times five). Five!

Well!

1. You didn't know Jane was out in Egypt too, did you?

2. Does your dad only fancy archaeologists?

3. Jane's obviously met your Mum Out There, or how would she know about Us? (Well, it could just about have been a C not a G, but I don't think it

meant Antony and Cleopatra – I mean, that's hardly hot news, is it? Especially in Egypt.) And why didn't your Mum say anything about Jane when she phoned?

4. Why's Jane writing to MY Dad?

MM, by the way, stands for Mary Mary. That's what Jane was on about in the postcard. Mary Mary Quite Contrary. That's what my Dad used to call Mum if he was trying to joke her out of a bad mood, and sometimes when she wasn't IN a bad mood, cos she wasn't really a moody person. And he'd always say, "How does your garden grow?" whenever she was doing the weeding.

(I used to call her Mary-Bear. Not ALL the time. When I was little, and sometimes when I was not-so-little (now please promise me that you will never, ever tell ANYONE about this – this is absolutely, classified, topper-than-top secret and I'm only telling you because you're my friend and I can trust you. Can't I?)

3 OF 5: MORE ABOUT WILFRED

Are you doing Wilfred for one of your Literature set texts, then? You must be doing a different exam board from us. I hope you like him. I think he's great.

Mum told me this next bit. She did Wilfred Owen for A-Level and read everything she could find about him. Did you know this? (If not, you can impress your English teacher with it.) Wilfred Owen died on 4th November 1918, exactly one week before the war ended. So just as all the church bells were ringing in Shrewsbury (where he lived – not far from here) and everyone was celebrating, his parents got the telegram to say he was dead.

Mum knew where he'd been killed, so when she and Dad were on their honeymoon in France she insisted on finding the place. It was on a canal, miles out in the countryside. A quiet, peaceful place, with mist and cows and grass and trees. But it wasn't peaceful back in 1918 – it was the front line. Wilfred and some others were trying to cross this canal, early in the morning, when they were shot. They're all buried together, at the back of an ordinary churchyard, and there's Wilfred's grave with all the others. Nothing special. Not WILFRED OWEN, BRILLIANT POET. Just another dead soldier. He was only twenty-five. And my Mum was standing there looking at his grave, and thinking: What a waste.

4 OF 5: JESS AND ME

It's nice, all that stuff you say about Jess and how I still love her, but it's not really true. It wasn't because of wanting her back that I was mad with Mark – it was because I was jealous, which is a much worse thing to have to say. Why jealous? Just because I didn't like the thought of the two of them being together and leaving me out. They might even talk about me! So you see, I'm much less worthy than you thought.

I once asked Mum how you know when you fall in love with someone. (You are being sworn to secrecy again here, because this isn't the sort of thing I'd ever ever talk about to someone like Mark.)

She said, "You just know. But you have to be careful. Because it can be misleading. It can be a bit like being mad." When I asked what that meant, she said, "You can lose all sense of reason. You think nothing matters except one person. And that's not necessarily a good thing to think."

And then she told me that falling in love is fantastic, but what matters more is loving someone in a more ordinary way. Like she loved Dad, she told me. "Living with them. With all their bad habits and their smelly socks and the things that irritate you. That's what love really is."And she said, "It's the way I love you, even though you've got some really disgusting habits, like . . ." (No! I'm not telling you that bit!)

Anyway, the point of all this is that I didn't love Jess. I liked her a lot. I still do. She's pretty and fun and she always brings crisps and chocolate to school. (I'm just a gannet, really.) And she doesn't spend hours worrying about what she looks like, like some girls do. She was my first ever girlfriend, so I'll always remember her, like my Dad remembers his first girlfriend. Her name was Annie and she was two years younger than him but six inches taller. She had the same reddish hair as him, and once someone asked if he was her little brother. I don't think Dad's ever got over that.

5 OF 5: EMBARRASSED OR WHAT?

And talking of Jess, it was all her fault, what happened in English today.

It was a weird coincidence, you telling me your middle name's Her-my-oh-knee. Did you know, Hermione's in this Shakespeare play called *The Winter's Tale*? It's the one we're doing for course work. There's this theatre workshop thing we're going to tomorrow, then we've got to write our Shakespeare essay in double-quick time cos all our course work's got to be finished a fortnight from now.

What happened was – Jess was sitting behind me, and she poked me in the back and whispered something about what was I doing at lunchtime, and I turned round and hissed back, "Oh yeah? You can make do with me when Mark's not available, is that what you think?" Then I heard, "Guy

Woodham" from the teacher, and suddenly everyone's looking at me.

Mrs Harman goes, "If you could *just* tear your attention away from the fascinating Miss McGoldrick –" (that's Jess) – "you would have heard me asking for a volunteer to read Hermione. As no one else seems to be offering, I think the part's yours."

That was mean. She *knows* I never volunteer to read stuff out. And there was all this sniggering, and I looked to see what page we were on and my heart sank, cos I had to do all these great long speeches. In case you don't know the story, what's happened is Hermione is a queen, and she was about to have a baby when the king got all jealous and thought it was his best friend's baby, not his, and he had Hermione flung in prison. Now she's on trial, and she's just had the baby and been dragged out of prison to stand up in court.

Well, I bet you're brilliant at reading Shakespeare, as you wanted to be Cleopatra, but I'm not. Specially with everyone listening and waiting for me to make an idiot of myself. Hermione says all this embarrassing stuff about having had her baby snatched from her breast and all that sort of thing. You can just imagine how all that went down. And Mrs Harman made me do the whole thing, and she kept saying, "With dignity, Guy, with dignity." You try speaking with dignity when your mates are cackling all round you like a parrot chorus. I got through it somehow, but my face was sizzling.

So Hermione isn't my favourite name, just at the moment. Sorry. But were you named after her, *The Winter's Tale* one? I've got to go and make something to eat now. For me and Mark, that is – he's still here. And by the way, he now admits to being a toad of the slimiest and wartiest kind. More tomorrow.

No news about Sharon or Manchester, but Dad's due back tomorrow and Guy the Griller will get to work.

I do hope you got past No.1. Or you won't be reading this anyway. And I hope you mail me TODAY to tell me what happened with the police.

Guy x

LEMME OUTA HERE!

Guy, my prince! You have got to rescue me. I pray that the electronic woodlouse I am attaching this message to can scuffle past the two-headed ogre on the gate and bring this to you before I swoon.

They are holding me in a tiny cell in the crumbling ruins of Gobbledygook Castle. It is freezing cold. Monster icicles are growing off the ceiling. The walls are thick with slimy mould – it squelches and creeps around in the night. If you touch it your skin grows hairy warts. There is a skeleton hanging in chains above my head.His teeth chatter every time the wolf pack howls. Every now and then a bone drops off and Ginger tries to bury it in the spider dung. Oh no, the mad woman is wailing gain! "I only want to stroke your hair . . ." she keeps saying. I can hear her fingernails clawing at the bricks. I must eat. I must drink. But I don't think I can face it. All they give us are turnip cores and a saucer of their scurnmy bathwater. Shush! I hear footsteps. Someone's coming! The door is swinging open. They are bringing something in. Oh no, not more barbed wire!

Guy, my hero! Come for me,

SOON...
xxx

I KNOW WHO JANE IS!!!

Guy, this is urgent. The police haven't got me. I'm not in prison, really. I was pretending to be a Shakespearean Hermione flung into jail by the jealous king. Weird, that, isn't it? Hermione? King? Don't know if I was named after her but what I've got to tell you is spookily like *The Winter's Tale* and you had better sit down before you read it. It's sort of about my dad and yours – or rather your dad and my mum. I think they . . . Oh, I don't know where to *start*! Yesterday. Yes. I'll tell you from there.

It was mega-embarrassing when I went to tell Dad the police had been. He was busy chomping seed cake in Mrs Swanley's lounge. "Police?" he splattered, spraying seeds all over her yucca plant. "Eau!" went Mrs Swanley, fiddling with her pearls. "The Rozzers? The Flatfoots? The Dreaded Inquisition?" (It sounded like she was going through her CD collection.) "What can they want with yew, dear Franklin?" My dad picked a seed from a gap in his teeth, finished off his coffee and said he had absolutely no idea. He even had the cheek to say that it wouldn't surprise him if they weren't a couple of door-to-door salesmen and Annabelle was just "letting her imagination run riot as usual". So I told him that one of the "salesmen" looked dead mean and had shown me a card saying *Detective Inspector*. That made Dad twitch a bit. "Eau," went Mrs Swanley again, looking like she'd just smelled doggy pooh. Dad frowned and shook some cake crumbs off his trousers. He told Mrs Swanley he was sure it was all a big mistake but that he'd better go and find out what they wanted.

He wasn't exactly pleased to discover that I'd told the rozzers he'd gone into town. "You did what?!" he blasted, gripping my arm so hard it hurt. "Annabelle, you don't mess about with figures of authority! If they really were the police you could get me into serious trouble!" So I told him I was frightened they were going to arrest him and take him to prison and feed him turnips. And then he said a really horrible thing. I'm not even sure I want to repeat it "Oh, Annabelle!" he huffed. "You *silly, silly, silly little girl*!" I was so upset that I kicked a gnome into Mrs Swanley's pond. And Dad knew he'd done wrong because he kept calling out to me as I stomped off home: "Annabelle? Wait. I'm sorry. Annabelle?" But I wouldn't talk to him. Not until about an hour ago.

All that was yesterday, of course. When he got in from Mrs Swanley's he paced around for ages then yanked up the phone and called the police. I heard him going "Um, yes. Shopping trip, sorry. Um, station. Tomorrow? Yes, of course. Can I ask . . .? *Theft?* What kind of items? Well, I really don't know what that's got to do with . . .? What? Um, yes. Tomorrow." Then he banged the phone down and went to his study. And he didn't come out until tea that night. It was my turn to cook. We had courgette lasagne with dog food and peppers. At least one of us did. And he ate every bit.

Then today, while I was looking through Woodham's pick-your-own mail, he announced he had to go out. "The police station," he said "to help those detectives with some . . . inquiries." I kept my back to him all the time. He stroked my shoulder, then he was gone.

While he was out I read your message and wrote my first reply "from prison". I made it as silly as I possibly could to stop me thinking about proper prison and whatever it was that Dad could have done. I was really frightened and cried while I was doing it. I just wanted someone to come and hold me and tell me in the nicest possible way that I was their precious little girl and it was all going to turn out all right in the end. I wanted a Mary-Bear hug.

And that was when I started to think about Jane, and began to get really mad. So mad that I started pulling knickers and socks and stuff from my drawers and chucking them all over the bedroom floor. I was wading through tights when the door banged to. I flew downstairs. Dad was in the kitchen. "Well?" I shouted. He yanked the fridge open, flipped the ring off a can of lager and started to guzzle. "Oh," he said grumpily. "We're talking again, are we?" I snatched a bit of kitchen roll and blew my nose. "What have you done?!" I demanded. "Do I have to go into care or what?" (Just to make the point, I stamped my foot.) He sighed and stared out of the window. "I haven't done anything," he muttered tiredly. "Stop being so melodramatic." So I reminded him he'd just been to see the police. "It was something to do with your mother's work," he said. "MUM?" I shouted. "What's she got to do with it?" He rubbed his brow and looked a bit worried. "Nothing," he said. But I could tell by the way he gritted his teeth that he'd said the wrong thing and was only trying to fob me off. So I said. "It's something to do with that locket, isn't it?" He clamped his teeth even tighter and sighed. "Annabelle, please forget you ever saw that locket."

No chance. “Where did it come from?” I asked. “Never mind where it came from!” he said, getting angry. “Just promise me you won’t say another word about it. All will be revealed when your mother finally drags herself back to these shores.”

So then I thought, OK, Daddykins, if I can’t talk about the locket, let’s talk about your girlfriend – and I said “Why do you only fancy archaeologists, Daddy? What’s so special about them?” He screwed up his face. ‘What are you wittering on about now?”

I grabbed a bunch of grapes and started lobbing them at him. “Does Mum know your girlfriend’s working with her?” A grape hit him plop on the end of the nose. “Annabelle,” he said (very, very quietly), “pack that in,or I shall do something to you that I probably should have done several years ago.” I threw another grape (but deliberately missed). “Annabelle!” he roared. “I’ve had a long and exhausting afternoon. Will you please explain what this is about?” “JANE!” I roared back. “Your hussy! Your TART. The one who’s sending cards to –”

But by now he had stormed across the room. Cripes, Guy. I really thought I was going to get it. He squeezed his can and a geyser of lager nearly hit the ceiling. “Stop that this instant,” he shouted. “I will not have talk like that in the house! Especially not about your mother.” Somewhere in the garden, Ginger woofed. "I didn't say Mum, I said Jane!" I shouted. He swung around, spraying lager everywhere. "Oh, for goodness' sake, child. Jane *is* your mother!"

Ginger woofed again. The grapes dropped out of my hands. My bottom lip started to jump. "Who's Mum then?" I said. He dragged a hand across his mouth. "Sit down," he said. I sank like a stone. "You're horrible," I wailed. "Guy said there was something funny going on." Dad nodded like his head was stuck on a spring. "I might have known Master Woodham was involved in this." "You leave Guy alone!" I barked – and so did Ginger. He pawed at the door. Dad and I yelled, "Quiet!" Ginger woofed again. Dad ignored him and leaned across the table. "Annabelle, Jane was your mother's pet name, once. At York, she called herself Mary Jane so she wouldn't be confused with Guy's mother. Everyone liked it and it stuck, that's all. I was teasing you about it on the way back from the doctor's.There is nothing more to it than that."

He put out a hand to touch my hair. But I pulled away quickly. My head was spinning. "Well, I've never heard you call her Jane!" He backed off with an idle shrug. "People grow out of these things. After college, when we went our separate ways, there was no need to keep it up any more. If you want to know the absolute truth what really made her drop it was when someone remarked that "Mary Jane" is a name for a particularly demure type of shoe. There are a great many words to describe your mother but demure most certainly would not be one of them." "I hate you!" I snapped, whipping round in my seat. He lifted a finger to give me a lecture, but Ginger started whining again and Dad turned his anger on him instead. "That flipping mutt," he grumbled, peering through the window.

And it was then I started thinking things, like why were there five big sloppy xs from Mary Jane to Tom on that card? Perhaps I shouldn't have said it, but I did: "What about Guy's father? Did *he* drop it?" Ginger woofed and woofed. Dad narrowed his gaze. "What's that supposed to mean? What's Tom got to do with any of this?" I went to the sink to wash my face. "Do you see him a lot? Does . . . Mum see him a lot?" Dad shrugged again. "What are you talking about? What exactly has Guy been saying?" "Nothing," I said. Ginger whined and scratched and whined again. "Oh, what *is* the matter with that dog?" Dad griped. And finally, he yanked the door open. "Oh my God," he gasped. I ran to the door. Ginger was there, wagging his tail. He put his nose to the floor . . . and nuzzled Jupiter.

He is alive but very weak. We don't know yet whether he crawled to the door hoping there would be a guinea-pig flap or if Ginger found him somewhere and brought him home. It ended my talk with Dad, anyway. I don't know what to say. I'm not sure I should have told you this. Guy, what are they doing? What have we found? I'm not sure I like it. Please write soon.

Annabewildered
XXXXX

DON'T PANIC!

Dear Crazy Annabelle,

I wish you'd e-mailed straight away yesterday. I HATE the thought of you crying and frightened and in the house alone, and imagining all those gruesome things about prison. If I'd been there you could have had a great big Guy the Gorilla hug. I was late in from school today cos of the trip, but I logged on straight away and couldn't believe you hadn't sent me anything new. We can stay online and mail each other all evening if you want to. If you ask me, it would serve both our Dads right if we clocked up a gigantic phone bill. I'm waiting to get my gorilla mitts on mine as soon as he gets in later tonight.

You didn't REALLY make him eat dog food, did you? What flavour?

Woodlouse, by the way, is what Mark calls me when we argue, which is fairly often. I call him Miff, cos his name is Mark Ian Findlay. Anyway, there are more serious things to talk about than woodlice and dog food. You must have been frantic when you thought your Dad was about to be clapped in jail. But "helping the police with their inquiries" probably means just that, doesn't it? I can't believe your parents would do anything criminal. I mean, your Dad's an Oxford Don. (I've never really known what that meant. Only that it sounds Really Important. Does he walk about with one of those mortar board things on his head? If so, it must be really difficult to keep it on, especially when its windy. He doesn't wear it at home, does he?)

But seriously. If it's something about the locket, then I bet it's just some daft mistake that will be cleared up as soon as your Mum gets home.

Talking of whom – Why were we so daft about the Jane business? It seems obvious now, only a bit mean of your Dad for winding you up like that. But I've read what you said about the argument with your Dad, at least three times, and I think you must be getting it a bit exaggerated. About your-Mum-alias-Jane and my Dad, I mean. They were all friends, weren't they? And friends can send each other xs – I mean, we do. It was just a friendly way of keeping in touch, wasn't it? Dad must have told them, you know, about Mum. That was one of the awful things, telling everyone. He had to spend evening after evening phoning people and writing to them and all these cards and letters kept coming and it was awful. All that sympathy. Your parents might even have been at the funeral for all I know. Dad had to make a real effort to be nice to everyone but all I could do was stare at the ground. I wouldn't have noticed if Frankenstein's monster had been there.

More cheerful topic. The trip I told you about was to the theatre at Stratford-upon-Avon. It was great. They showed us around the backstage area and we saw all sorts of costumes and props, and we had a workshop on *The Winter's Tale*, with real actors. At lunchtime a group of us went down to look at the canal basin and the lock gates. There were all these narrow boats in the basin, and one of them's a café. While we were watching a couple of people heaving at the lock gates to get their boat out on to the river, I suddenly had a funny feeling. I looked at the lockgates with the theatre behind, across the grass, and I remembered seeing this photo in Mum's album, of the very same place. So as soon as I got home, I looked to check. It's the same place all right. In the photo, Mum and Dad are standing by the lock gates, and my Mum's pregnant, in fact so pregnant that she must have her bag packed at home ready to go to hospital. To have ME! And my

Dad's got his arm round her, and they're both looking really happy. When I saw the photo, it made me go all funny and blurry. I expect this sounds daft, but I thought – well, I didn't know I'd been to Stratford before, but there I am in the picture, not even born yet.

Good old Jupiter for turning up – I hope he's got over whatever happened to him.

I'll be late home tomorrow cos of rugby practice (you didn't know I had rugby in common with your Dad, did you?) so I'll be a bit later than usual. But please e-mail me tonight! And PLEASE tell me next time you're on your own and upset, if it happens. I would like to know.

Guy xxx

PLOT THICKENS AGAIN

Dear Annabelle,

OK, here goes. It's late but I've just got to tell you.

First, Manchester. When I asked Dad how it went, he said, "Oh, so-so." I was hawk-eyed for any signs of shiftiness or guilt. "How were things at the Manchester office?" I asked, dead casual.

Guess what he said!

"We haven't got a Manchester office." So I said, all accusing, "But that's where you told me you were going!" I mean, couldn't he even invent a fake story and stick to it? But he said, "No, you lemon, it's our CLIENT'S Manchester office," and he gave me all this authentic-sounding spiel that made me think I must have got it wrong the first time – all about them transferring their accounts to a new system and needing someone to sort it out so that it made sense. So I had to back off a bit.And, just now when I came up to bed (Dad's crashed out after the car journey from hell) I checked his e-malls and he'd already read and trashed one from Sharon. It turns out I've got that wrong too, at least partly – Sharon was someone who knew Mum and Dad ages ago and they just thought it would be nice to meet. I won't send you her whole message but I've done a cut-and-paste. Here's what she says;

> I enjoyed our meal, but I really can't be an agony
> aunt for you. If what you need is bereavement
> counselling, then you should find a specialist.

And she talks a bit about how awful she felt when her father died last year. Then:

> Did you find it as strange as I did, meeting in
> person when we'd only communicated by e-
> mail? I think we'd both underestimated the
> potential for disappointment, to be honest. The
> problem with e-mail is that you can make
> yourself sound like a different person – I think,
> under normal circumstances, that's half the fun.
> But our circumstances aren't really normal, are

> they? So I'm sorry that it didn't work out, Tom,
> but thanks for giving it a go.

And then she says things about always remembering Mum and what a terrible pity IT all was.

If Dad ever finds out I've read this, let alone sent it to you, he'll murder me. Bits of me will be shredded, cooked and eaten. So *please* erase it from your memory just in case you're ever hypnotized!

Secondly, about that Stratford photo I told you about. When Dad got in, whacked out though he was, I shoved it under his nose and told him I'd been there today. Then it occurred to me to ask who took the photo?

GUESS?

"Franklin," he said. "Annabelle's Dad. We went to Stratford together, the three of us." So I asked, "Didn't Annabelle's Mum go?" He ummed and aahed and said,"Well, no, otherwise she'd have been in the photo, wouldn't she? I can't remember why not." So then I asked him, all casual again (I'm getting quite good at this), "How long is it since you've seen them, then? Franklin and Jane?" He looked a bit embarrassed. "We sort of lost touch," he went. So I said, "Did they come to the funeral?" He gave me a pained look for using the F-word. Then he said, "Jane did," and it was like he could only just about get the words out.

But I kept on going. I said, "What, on her own? Why didn't Franklin come, if you were all such good friends?" He just clamped his lips together and shook his head. I waited, but nothing came out. So I asked him, "What happened since York, then? Did you have an argument or something?" And he said, "Not exactly. Now if you don't mind, Guy, I've had a very long day and I'd like to crash out in front of the TV."

I knew it was really cos he wanted to shut me up, but I let him crash, and fetched him the pasta I'd cooked (no dog food – if we had a dog I'd have given him some) and then VERY VERY casually gave him the Egypt postcard and said, "Oh, by the way, this came."

When he looked at it, he sort of stiffened. "I take it you've read it?" he said. I told him it's quite difficult NOT to read a postcard, I mean it's not like opening someone else's letters on purpose. Then I said, "Looks like Jane wants to stay friends, at least. Are you going to meet her? When?" He just grunted and pretended to be engrossed in the ram-headed sphinx.

So, is this progress or a blind alley? See what your dad's got to say about Stratford-upon-Avon.

By the way, I haven't forgotten about Caverner Road and the pancakes. I didn't think there was a good moment tonight, that's all.

Still no e-mail from you today. Are you all right?

Your sleuthing partner,
Guy

I KNOW ITS LATE BUT . . .

Dear Annabelle,

I forgot to tell you about Jess and me today. No, that's not true. I didn't forget. I wasn't going to tell you. But now I am, cos it's late and I can't sleep.

When I went down to look at the canal boats, it was with Jess. Earlier I told you there was a group of us, and it's true. But then Jess and I sort of strayed away from the group. It wasn't me that made it happen. It was like those sheepdog trials on TV when a couple of sheep get singled out from the flock.

Jess said, "I suppose you've heard – Mark and I aren't going out any more?" "Oh, yeah," I said. Actually, I hadn't, but I made it sound like no big deal – even though I was dying to know why not, and who broke it off. But I can ask Mark those things. "Are you seeing anyone now?" she said, and I said No. "Oh," she said. "Well, Mark says you've got a new girlfriend." "Have I?" I said, playing for time. "Yes," she said. "Some one you talk to by e-mail."

Annabelle – to be honest, the first thing that came into my head was, "Annabelle's not a girlfriend. She's just a friend" But I didn't say that. What I said was, "That's right. Annabelle. She's great." (And I said some more things that I'm not telling you, cos they'd make you big-headed.)

And then Jess got really annoyed. Not exactly because of you, but because of the e-mail. She said, "That's crazy. How can you feel like that about someone you haven't ever really talked to? Someone you haven't even seen?" And I told her, "I don't know. I just do, that's all."

I hope you don't mind, and I shall regret sending this as soon as I click on Send, but here goes –

ROCKET TAKES OFF

Dear Huggable,

Last night I had a peculiar dream. It started with my dad, all dressed up in a leopard-skin outfit. He was swinging one-handed off Mrs Swanley's arch, beating his chest with his other hand and screeching like a chimpanzee. Suddenly, Mrs Swanley came out with a bucket. I thought she was going to chuck water all over him (I would have), but she didn't. She put the bucket on her head, threw her arms out wide and shouted, "Franklin. I'm yours!" My dad grunted back "Me Tarzan, you Jane!" And

Mrs Swanley clanked: "No! I'm Eleanor! But Franklin, my dear, I don't *give* a damn!" Which is what Mum says sometimes when she's arguing with Dad, but I've never found out why.

And then Mum was in the dream. She came walking towards me out of a sandstorm. She had something in her arms and I was *sure* it was a baby. A dark-haired baby boy. I felt myself go prickly inside. But the closer she got, the smaller and smaller the baby became. Until it wasn't a baby at all – it was the locket. Mum flipped it open. Inside were two pictures: but I couldn't see who they were. But I saw our middle names: Alexander and Hermione. "But Mum," I said, "what does it mean?" She waved at me then and started to fade. "Mum!" I shouted after her. "Mum, come back!" But she was gone and something else was rising from the sand. It was lying on its tummy, looking proudly across the desert. I thought it was the Sphinx at first, but when I looked closer it wasn't . . . it was Hornbeam.

A sandy tear rolled down my cheek. The tear dripped on to Hornbeam's paw. He turned his stony neck and bent down slowly and licked the paw clean. His eyes were made of shining jewels and a desert storm whistled out of his mouth. Then I *thought* I woke up, because I opened my eyes, I'm *sure* I did, and saw little Rocket sitting on my chest. He made a silent miaow then turned and jumped off me in a blurry trail of silver-grey fur. I watched his tail swish out of the door. It was just like he wanted me to follow him somewhere – and then I did wake up, and found a single white whisker on my duvet.

But no Rocket.

This morning he is nowhere to be found. Guy, I'm really worried. He has gone missing twice before, but usually if I go round the house rattling the can opener there will be a feeble scratching in the airing cupboard or something. Dad is feeling rather guilty. He thinks – huh, *thinks* – Rocket might have "slipped out" when he put the car away last night. I have sent Dad out to comb the streets. I would have gone, too, but I don't think I could bear it if we found poor Rocket's broken little body lying in a pool of blood in a gutter. Dad has advised me to do "something useful" while the search is on. "Mail Guy," he said. Hmph. That's the only decent thing he's said in days. So here I am. Please have a digital shoulder ready. There may be bad news at any moment. I might have to ask you to keep to your pledge of mailing me or CALLING me (did you lose my number? It's 01865 11207) the next time I'm sad or lonesome.

Pressing Send now . . .

SHAKESPEARE AND SANTA

Hi, I'm here again, typing while they dredge the lake. OK I know. That was OTT. I'm just trying to be brave. It would be awful now that Jupiter is back and taking light exercise on his wheel to lose my beautiful kitten. I couldn't bear it.

Type, must type.

At breakfast this morning, I asked Mardy Guts about your Stratford photo. He just got even mardier and said. "Annabelle, you can't expect me to remember things from fifteen years ago. You'll be asking me next what play we went to see! And I have no idea why 'Jane' wasn't with us. She'd probably gone pot-holing or something that day. She's a very independent woman, your mother." So I said, "Is that why she went to Guy's mum's funeral without you, then?" He jabbed his fork into a piece of bacon and started sawing like mad with his knife. "I don't know *what* you're driving at with all these ridiculous questions, but I sincerely wish you'd change the tune." So I did. I said, "Do you ever wear your mortar in bed, *Daddy*?" and ran for it before he could do something nasty.

He's been acting really weird these past few days. There's definitely something funny going on in this house. Yesterday afternoon I came in early from school because netball practice was cancelled – and caught him with his head up the dining-room chimney. Honest. I'm not kidding. Our fireplaces are ancient and the one in the dining-room is loosely boarded up. He'd ripped the wood away and was ferreting about up the fluey thingy. There was soot EVERYWHERE. Ginger came padding in and got it on his paws and poddled it all over the dining-room carpet. Mum'll go spare when she finds out.

Anyway, I said to him, "Dad, what are you doing? I know it's you who brings the presents at Christmas, I found out when I was six. Why are you playing at Santa Claus?" Pulling out of the chimney he banged his head on the bricks and a pile more soot fell into the grate."What are you doing home so early?" he snapped. I folded my arms, cocked my hip and gave him my very best girl-power GLARE (he really hates that pose). "I thought I heard a pigeon flapping about," he said.
Oh yeah. Totally believable, Dad. So I said, "Is that your secret hiding-place, then?" Huh. He might have looked like he'd just come home from the pit but I could tell his cheeks were glowing red. "It's not me who's –" he began, prodding a finger in his chest (and leaving soot all over his shirt). Then he changed his mind and griped: "Haven't you got any homework to do?" I slung my school bag over my shoulder, rubbed my toe in a patch of soot and said, "Haven't you got any *housework* to do?" He just grimaced and threw a brick end into the

chimney. And another lot of soot came plopping down.

He's mental. There's no other explanation for it. He's just in such a MOOD. And he accuses me of getting tetchy! Just before he went out looking for Rocket, the phone rang. I went hurtling to the lounge, only to find he'd got there first. He grunted something then put the phone down. "Who was it?" I asked. "Wrong number," he muttered, peeking through a crack in the curtains. He's been doing that a lot since the police came round. And writing down the numbers of parked cars. I think he thinks we're being watched. I said. "Are you sure it was a wrong number? I'm expecting a call from Guy."

He just exploded.

"I think I know my own number by now," he snapped. "And if you think you're going to go clocking up a string of calls to Herefordshire, my girl, you can think again! What's Guy Woodham ringing you for, anyway?" I told him it was none of his business. But stupidly I blurted. "I never ask you about your girlfriends, do I?" He knotted his eyebrows and gave me one of his scowly looks. I thought he was going to start ranting on about Mrs Swanley or the woman from the bread shop, but instead he said, "Are you trying to tell me that you and Guy are . . .?" He snorted a laugh and didn't finish. I snatched up a cushion and hugged it to my chest. "So?" I pouted. 'What if we are?" He rubbed one hand across the side of his neck "No," he laughed, "That's not possible. Not after . . ." "Not after what?" I demanded. But he just got huffy and said if I wanted him to find "this cat" I had better move out of the way. "Guy's my boyfriend now," I said. "I want you to take me to his house to see him." And he gave me this distant, painful look – as if he was feeling like you did at Stratford, looking back miles and miles into the past. "I'll try around the back field first," he said, then shoved me aside and that was that.

I hate him. He deserves to eat dog food the rest of his life. And I really DID put it in his lasagne. Prime chicken cuts in marrowbone jelly. Ginger had the minced beef with parmesan cheese.

This is terrible. Eleven-twenty am. Where *is* Rocket? Where is Dad? Sending again. If you hear the beep, please mail straight back and comfort me. I'm getting a bit sniffy. Here it comes . . .

TWO SECRETS

Dab, dab. That was me with the tissues. I guess you're not there, so I'll just ramble on if that's OK.

I know I shouldn't have told Dad that you're my boyfriend, but after what you wrote last night I just couldn't help it. It popped out. Sorry.

NO! Poodles! I'm NOT sorry! I want to be your girl-friend. There. I've said it. Of course I don't mind you telling Jess how great I am. Maybe she'll stop trying to get back with you now. Why can't she just stay DUMPED! It's all right for her, having you there, tickling your chin with a buttercup by the lock gates, telling you you're crackers fancying someone you've never seen. Well pooh to her. Pooh to all the Jesses and Sharons and Dads. I'm fed up of people droning on about how we can't possibly feel for each other because we've never met! We have met. We talk to each other nearly every day, don't we? And I don't care what Sharon says. I know you can make yourself sound like another person by e-mail. But if that was right, why would I have told you things I didn't have to? Like when I mixed up Jane and Tess? And why would you have told me about Jess at the canal? It's because we're being truthful with each other, isn't it? There might be some things I haven't exactly told you, but only because you've never asked. In case you're wondering, here are two of them . . .

1. I *do* talk about you now with Laura Blackman.She *is* my best girly friend in the world. I haven't shown her your letters, but I tell her what you say. She's seen your picture. She is soooo jealous. She thinks you're really DDG (that's drop-dead gorgeous) and keeps going on about how I should ring you and get a proper date. I keep

telling her she's stupid cos you're miles away and that it's up to you to make the first move, anyway. Laura just says if she had a yunk (top word, now) like you on the line she wouldn't hang about for "someone" to steal you. She says I should definitely call if Jess makes any more moves on you. That was before your letter last night. I keep looking at the phone and wondering . . .

2. This bit's harder to write. Please don't hate me. It wasn't my fault. I know I should have told you way back when, but . . . It's about me and another boy.

When our server crashed that time, I was clumping around school in a really grotty mood and this boy, Steven Inkler, wanted to know why I was kicking lumps out of a desk in the computer lab. No one talks to Stinkler because he's a nerd. He wears sandals to school and if he went out in the sun with a burger on his head it would fry in his greasy hair in less time than it takes to boil a Phiggins egg. Anyway, I was ranting on about our server being down and how I desperately needed to type a message to my very best friend in the world and he said, "So? Why don't you type your info into a word processing package then import it from a floppy when your server's back up?" I huffed and flicked my hair back out of my eyes – and Stinkler grinned. "Don't know how to, do you?" he toadied. So I told him his breath smelt worse than our dustbin and he smirked and said. "Would you like me to show you?"

Agh! Shiveroony! It was awful, being at Stinker's mercy. But I had to. I was desperate. So I plonked myself down at a PC and said. "All right, dog breath, which button do I press?" He put his mouth to my ear and whispered, "Ah, ah, not before you make me a promise." "SUCH AS???" I snapped. And he smirked again.

Guy, I am not going to tell you what I had to let him do because it was meaningless and it will NEVER, EVER happen again. I would not have given in if I hadn't been so desperate. And if Tracey Scudding ever tells you I enjoyed it, she is a lying WITCH, OK? The worst of it is, when I got home that night our server was still down and do you know what Dad said? "Look, Annabelle, if you're really that frantic, type your message into the word processor and I'll show you how to import it into . . ." AGHHHH! Dad knew what to do all the time. I could have avoided Stinkler altogether and not have to wear my collar up for the next – Hang on, phone call.

Mrs Swanley, not you. Gotta go. She's phoning from her mobile at the bottom of her garden to say that something's making noises in our garden shed. Please let it be Rocket. Will let you know,

A
xxx

PS That's a very sad story about Wilfred Owen. I told Ms Spence and she went into raptures! She was “delighted to see I was doing some background research” and promised to get me a book about it. Great.

PPS If you really want me to be your girlfriend I will require a full list of your disgusting habits.

MM

Guy. Oh help. I’ve just come back from the garden shed. You *must* ring today between two and six p.m. Dad will be out at rugby. We need to talk. This is urgent. Honestly, this is NOT a joke! I have just found Rocket. He WAS in the shed. But there was something else, too. It was on a shelf with some gardening books. I only saw it cos Rocket had got tangled in some old green netting and I nearly bashed my nose on the shelf trying to free him. It’s a book of Wilfred Owen poems. At first I was sort of pleased, because you know we are doing Wilfred Owen at the moment – but then I opened it up. Guy, you had better get ready for this. Inside was a message, this is what it said

Happy birthday my darling Franklin.
Love you now and for ever
Mary Mary (still contrary) x

Mary Mary, not Mary Jane. Guy, if you think this means what I think this means you had better call me.

Help,
A

Dear Annabelle,

Let me get this right. You think that message in the book means my Mum loved your Dad. Or else you think she was having an affair with him after she was married to MY Dad.

No, you've got it wrong. You must have. This is my Mum you're talking about. Not someone in a soap.

Why don't you ask Franklin? He didn't even go to her funeral, remember. That's how much he cared.

Guy

PS I hope Rocket turns up.

UNHAPPY & FRIGHTENED

Guy,

Don't be horrible. And don't be huffy. I'm only telling you what I've found. I never said your mum loved my dad or anything like it. And it's not fair to ask me to ask my dad something like that. I'm scared to. I don't know what he would do. I know you don't believe me or want to believe me, that's why I've scanned what MM wrote and attached it to this message. See for yourself.

And I *told* you Rocket was in the garden shed, tangled up in some netting. Or are you so mad at me now you can't even be bothered to read my letters properly or remember how upset I was about my kitten?

Annabelle

PS I keep picking up my phone and it seems we still have a *dialling tone* . . .

PEACE MISSIVE

Dear Annaballistic,

All right. Sorry. I didn't mean to be horrible or huffy and I did read your message properly – I just got confused and wasn't thinking straight, that's all. Because of what was in the book. I'm sorry you are unhappy and frightened, especially if it was my fault. It wasn't your fault for passing on what you found.

My Mum and your Dad. When you thought it was MY Dad and YOUR Mum, I said you were exaggerating it all, didn't I? But I can't say that this time. It made me feel so peculiar, seeing that message in her own handwriting. I mean, that's my Mum. Writing to your Dad. She must have had this whole secret life I knew nothing about.

She loved him.

When did it happen?

How long for?

WHAT happened?

Why did they both end up with different people? Or did this happen AFTER they'd both married different people? I want to ask her! I want to know!

I've read in mountaineering books about people walking over crevasses. They're on what they think is snow over solid rock. It's not. The snow gives way underneath them and they fall though and keep falling. Now I know how that must feel.

I can't ask her, so you'll have to ask HIM. Franklin. Franklinstein. Dr King. He's the only person who can tell us. He loved her too, didn't he. I've been reading all your messages, and seeing that it all makes sense. Thing she's said. Things he's NOT said. Annabelle, I think we're finding out something we'd rather not know.

But we can't stop now, can we?

It was really weird last night. I couldn't sleep for thinking about my Mum and your Dad, and then I started half-dreaming about your dream, the one about that locket with both our middle names in it. Like someone was swinging it in front of my eyes to try to hypnotize me. Alexander and Hermione. And then suddenly I was wide awake again. Thinking about the three of them going to the theatre. Your Dad, my Mum, my Dad. My Mum nine months pregnant. One pregnant woman, two men. Just like in the play, *The Winter's Tale*. That was the scene they did for us in the workshop, where Hermione's husband gets raving jealous. Your Dad, my Mum, my Dad. I told you my Dad was jealous of yours, and this is why.

He *knew*.

I'm really glad you've got Rocket back as well as Jupiter. Sorry for being Gorilla-ish. And I'll log on again later in case you send me a message back.

Guy

TEARING AND KICKING

Dear Guy,

Once upon a time there was this strange little locket, with the names of Alexander and Hermione in it . . .

And now there is . . .

Oh. I'll tell you in a minute. First, I have got to tell you this. Don't be mad, cos it might be important. It's another bit I missed from my KRASHERAMA message when I had to log off because of . . . you know, being silly. I just forgot all about it. Stupid, stupid Annabelle. It's more from Dad and me in the car. Remember I got stroppy and asked him why they wanted us to be e-mail pals? This is what he said: "When Mary died, Guy became very bitter and depressed." "I know," I said, frowning, "he had to have counselling." Dad nodded and turned a corner. "One night, just after Christmas, I had to ring Tom about . . . some financial matter or other, and he started to talk about . . . her. It. The funeral. You know."

No. I didn't know then. I didn't know he was madly in love with *your mum*. I remember I tried to look him in the eye, but he was screwing up his face as if he'd sat on a nettle. Guilty or what? Then he said, "Anyway, Tom was worried that Guy was becoming too insular and lonely. So we decided that if someone wrote to Guy, someone . . . fizzy, like you –" "FIZZY?" I shouted. Dad jumped so much he nearly swerved into some cones – "that Guy might come out of his shell a bit more and start leading a normal life again."

Is this our "normal" lives, Guy? The two of us snooping round looking for love letters and photos from one parent to another? Cos that's what I've been doing. And I hate myself. I feel like I'm having a horrible nightmare, kicking and tearing my bedclothes off, then my night-dress and then my skin. Tearing and kicking. Looking for the truth. Looking through all the albums I can find. Looking for pictures of your lovely mum and the woman magnet I call my dad.

Guy, I can't possibly ask about this. Even I can't look him in the eye and say, "Which did you prefer, then? Mary Mary or Mary Jane?" He'll slap me across the face, I know. He'll call me a stupid, interfering little girl. All for discovering his secret in the shed, and the even bigger secret he keeps in his jacket. Tonight, he asked me to go and buy chips. Chips, because he's too lazy to boil potatoes. Too much on his mind to make our tea. "There's no money in the shopping tin," I huffed. He pinched his eyebrows and wafted a hand. "Wallet, in the study. Take a flyer from that."

The one place I hadn't looked: the place where dads keep cute little pictures of their cute little "families". I saw a corner of a photo there. One little corner. Two little corners. I pulled the pictures out. One was of me, seven years old, braces on my teeth, pony-tailed hair, cute as you like; the other was your mum, on a fairground ride. Mary Mary on the dancing horses.

My dad keeps a picture of *your* mum in his wallet.

I despise him. Totally. But I'm not going to tell him. Not right now. Not while I'm all confused and swimming. I'm going to wait till Mum comes home. I'm going to keep on gathering the evidence.

Like this . . . I was doing my homework on the dining-room table, and he came in pretending to look for something. "What are you up to tonight?" he said, obviously trying to smooth things a bit. "What does it look like?" I mumbled, keeping my head down and scratching away. "A poem, if I'm not mistaken," he said. I spun round in my chair and covered it over. (It was a poem, we have to write one now.) "What's the big deal?" he laughed. "You've always let me see your English before." That's true. I have. But this poem was . . . personal.

Anyway, then I got really mad and thought, I'll show you something *poetic*, Daddy. I reached into my bag and brought out the Wilfred Owen book. His face went GREY. "I found this in the garden shed," I said. "I borrowed it. I hope you don't mind. We're doing Wilfred Owen at school at the moment. Do you like him?" He gripped the back of a chair. "Yes," he said quietly. "Yes, I do." I forced a little smile. "Annabelle –" he started, but I cut him off. "Guy told me his mum liked Wilfred Owen. That's interesting, isn't it?" He rubbed his hand across his mouth a few times. Then I got him with something that really made him wobble. "Dad, you know about Shakespeare, don't you?" He shrugged, feebly. "Yes, of course." I ever so casually screwed the top back on to my pen. "Guy says there's a character called Hermione in *The Winter's Tale.*" "Oh God," he muttered, and turned away. "Have you seen it?" I asked. "Is that the play you saw at Stratford when you took that photo of Mary and Tom?" He grimaced and ran his hands through his hair. "I – yes. Possibly. Yes." So I said, "Am I named after her? Hermione, I mean? Is she like me? A tenacious firebrand?" He gritted his teeth and let out a sigh. Then he whipped round and picked up the Wilfred Owen. "Have you read this?" he said, tightening his lips. I shook my head. He seemed relieved. He tapped it twice against his chin. "I'd like to borrow it back, if that's OK? Just for tonight. I . . . haven't been with Owen for a long, long time."

I had to look away then, try not to blob. "OK," I said. And he went to his study. Where he's been ever since.

Who cares? I've got the scan.

Talk to me soon.

I love you,
Annabelle
xxx

SHELL-SHOCKED

Dear Annabelle,

Your Dad was right about someone fizzy like you. You have fizzed me out of my shell. The only problem is that I'm about to crawl back into a new one and stay there.

Please don't say you love me, Annabelle, even though it made the computer screen fizzle in front of my eyes and my chair start to revolve, which is odd cos it's only an ordinary chair not a revolving one. No one's ever said that to me before. Except my Mum. And I don't know what to do about it.

And things are getting so complicated that I don't know who it is you think you love. I don't even know how to tell you this, and I can't ask my Dad because I'm too afraid of what he might say, but – here goes. Make sure you're sitting down and holding on to something.

I think they're keeping something from us. Something they're too afraid to talk about. Annabelle, suppose your Dad is my Dad too?

Suppose I'm your half-brother?

Best wishes,
Guy

NO! NO! NO!

A> It's me. I'm on-line. I just got your message.

I do not want to HEAR this. You CAN'T be my brother. You MUSTN'T be my brother. It's not possible. It's not . . .

NO! Guy Woodham, don't DO this to me! I'll never speak to you again if you EVER say anything HORRIBLE like that again.

I'm going to walk Ginger. I will look for your brain while I'm out. I think you must have left it up a mountain or something.

Oh, and BEST WISHES to you, TOO!

G> Wait!

I'm here. If you're still on-line, stay there . . .

It's *not* me doing it to you, is it? It's them.

But you *do* believe it, don't you? Because if you didn't, you'd have said, "Don't talk such tedious rubbish" or "Don't try to wind me up" or something like that.

Just think about it. They loved each other, didn't they? My Mum and your Dad. And he still loves her, doesn't he? Taking the Wilfred Owen book and shutting himself away with it. Keeping her photo in his wallet. Not a picture of *your Mum*.

What I don't understand is *when*. We know that your Dad went with my parents – no, I can't call them that anymore, it's too confusing. We know that Franklin went with Mary Mary and Tom to see *The Winter's Tale* at Stratford-upon-Avon just before I was born, say in July. But you were already born then. So your Mum (Mary Jane) probably wasn't pot-holing – she was more likely at home looking after a seven-month-old baby.

So the question is, when did Franklin and my Mum – you know, do it? I must have been conceived in the November just before you were born. So that means your Dad must have been having an affair with my Mum at the same time as waiting for his own baby daughter – you, that is – to be born in two months' time. That's a bit much, isn't it? I mean, is he a complete two-timing git or what?

A> Stop it! Stop it! STOP IT!

You don't understand. You CAN'T be my brother. Not then, not like the way you said. You just can't. And if you you keep on saying things like that about my dad, I'm going to pull the plug out.

Goodbye!

G> NO, HOLD ON!

What do you mean, I don't understand? You're probably right, I don't understand everything, but I also understand a bit too much.

For starters, there's this man I've shared a house with all my life. If what I've said is true, I'm living with a man who's no relation to me. He keeps me in his house and feeds me cos that's what he did when Mum was around, but now there's no need for him to have anything to do with me.

And what about this: your Dad suggested we start mailing each other, didn't he? He wants to keep in touch with his own son, especially now that I haven't got a Mum. And that time you got him to send an e-mail, when he said I was a fine young man and all that flannel. He was talking to me, his son. And that's why he doesn't like us getting – you know, a bit romantic. He hadn't thought of what he might be starting.

You've seen my photo and everyone always tells me I look like my Mum. No one ever says I look like my Dad – like Tom. Tom's got reddish-brown hair; mine's dark, like Mum's. Do I look like YOUR Dad?

Annabelle, you've GOT to think about this.

Please leave your plug in.

A> I don't *want* to think about this. Please, Guy, I don't want to lose you.

G> What do you mean? Lose me how?

A> Please don't make me say this.

G> Say what? Have you got even more surprises to spring on me? Have we got another couple of brothers and sisters, or a long-lost uncle whose name is Elvis Presley? You'll have to tell me now.

A> Look, just don't get mad at me, OK! I never meant it to happen like this. You can't be my brother the way you said – because I'm not seven months older than you. I'm not in Year Eleven. I'm not even in Year Ten. You never asked me, did you? Don't hate me. I'm in Year Nine. I'm fourteen years old. One, four, got it? Yes, a silly little girl with a crush on a senior.

NOW DO YOU UNDERSTAND?!

G>Yes.

A> Yes, what? Yes you understand or yes I'm a silly little girl - or both? And who's Elvis Presley?

A> . . . you hate me now, don't you?

A> Guy, are you still there? What does Yes mean?

G> It means Yes.

I was thinking about it, that's all. It's quite a big thing to get used to.

You lied to me, didn't you? About the netball photo, and how you'd grown since Year Nine? You let me go on thinking you were the same age, when we talked about mock exams and stuff. Why didn't you tell me? I thought I could trust you. And I thought you could trust me.

Anyway, it doesn't mean I'm not your brother, does it? It makes it more likely if anything. What I couldn't get my head round before was why the two babies (us) were born so close together. It makes more sense if there's a gap of a year and a half in between. Your Dad had me first, then he had you. I'm not making it all up. YOU were the one who found the Wilfred Owen book.

G> Annabelle, look, I'm sorry. One minute I think I've got a sister, next I've got a little sister. But I don't think you're silly, no. If I didn't think you were silly when you were my age, why should I think you're silly when you're younger?

G> Are you still there?

A> Yes, I'm still here. Don't be impatient. This isn't easy for me, either.

G> OK, but my dad – no, I mean Tom Woodham –

is going to go ballistic in a minute if he finds out what a phone bill I'm clocking up . . .

A> I had to go to the toilet. First this:

> You lied to me, didn't you? About the netball
> photo, and how you'd grown since Year Nine?
> You let me go on thinking you were the same
> age, when we talked about mock exams and
> stuff. Why didn't you tell me? I mean, I thought
>I could trust you.

I know. I'm sorry. And you *can* trust me. I had to keep pretending I was in Year Eleven because I was starting to like you then and I was frightened you'd go all huffy and ditch me. It's called cradle-snatching, Guy. You must get that.

I never did tell you why I haven't ever had a proper boyfriend. Dad says I scare them off too easily – boys of my own age, he means. He says I'm too intelligent and fizzy for them (hah hah). BOO! Are you scared, Guy Woodham? You should be. I am a tenacious firebrand, remember . . . and I'm absolutely crackers about you.

Oh, IT'S JUST NOT FAIR!!!

Don't you see, you're the first boy I've ever been able to talk to properly? And now you could be my horrible BIG brother. If you were here I'd beat you up! Oh, what are we going to do? Tell me, please. I can't ask Dad about this. I just can't.

Love,

A

G> I don't know what to say or think either. I mean, the ground's shifted under my feet, twice. First I'm not who I think I am. Then you're not quite who I thought you were, either.

But you are who I thought you were in all the important ways. I mean, we can talk to each other, like you say. That's nice. I could get used to having a sister.

And I never said it but I was RAVING MAD at that loathsome boy in the computer room. If I were there, you could hit me and I could hit him.

Are we going to tell them? Your Mum and our Dad and Tom Woodham?

A, I've got to log off now. He's just got home. TW, I mean.

Bye, Guy

JUST WASHING MY HANDS

Dear Guy,

I didn't go to school today. I woke up with a terrible headache and stayed in bed with the curtains closed. I felt miserable – after our messages, yesterday. I didn't want to see or be with anyone. Not even my poor little Rocket. He cried and scratched at my door for ages. I wrapped my pillow round my head and tried to shut him out, but it sounded like his claws were coming through the stuffing and scratching the thoughts right out of my brain. Horrible, ugly, depressing thoughts. I have never felt like this before. Not ever.

But in some ways it's a wonderful day. A happy sad funny sort of yippee kind of day. I don't want to tell you why just yet. I haven't gone mad. You don't have to worry. My fizz has gone a little bit flat, but I'm still all here – you know, with it. And I am still talking to you, aren't I? We have that, don't we? No one can take that away from us. You will always talk to me, won't you, Guy? Even when I'm not there? Like you did to that squirrel? Did he ever tell you what colour my eyes were? Too busy chewing a nut, I suppose.

Did I ever tell you what my mum said once? When I was ten and I dropped my favourite cup on the floor and smashed it into a zillion pieces? She said, "Everything happens to a purpose, A. Put your trust in the Universe. The Universe knows what it's doing, child." And I thought she was a lot more cracked than my cup. But now I'm not so sure . . .

It's just so FUNNY, really. Before he went to work, Dad wanted to call in Doctor Keelan. I didn't tell him I had a headache. I fibbed and said I had period pain and that Doctor Keelan wouldn't love him any more if he dragged her out for "girly trouble". That made him really huffy, of course. "You and I need to talk," he said. He was standing by the bedroom window with his hands in his pockets, looking at the world all grim and serious and deadly dadly. "There are certain things we need to discuss."

Things to discuss. Oh yes, we have things. I should have said, "Like my brother, you mean?" But I didn't. I couldn't. The words wouldn't come. So I reminded him about my ovaries and eggs and phases of the moon and he muttered something mean about Mum being away and said he would ask Mrs Swanley to pop in.

She couldn't get round here quickly enough.

She hoovered and dusted, did a bit of washing, gave Ginger a whole can of food to eat (honestly, Guy, he looks like a *barge*) and best of all, she cleaned the loo. "I think you have a problem with your cistern," she fluted. "I had to pull five times before it would work. It's making a funny sort of clunking noise. As if something is rattling around in there. Better tell your father when he comes home tonight." Then she put a hand on my thumping head and asked would I like to hear a story! As if I was five years old or something! I wanted to say, "Why don't you just go and swing from your trellis!" But I didn't, I excused myself and went to the loo.

When I came back she had to ask me three times

was I feeling all right. A sickly grin, she said I had. She was definitely right about the grin. I said, "Mrs Swanley, I would never have believed it before, but even you have a purpose in the Universe. . ." She fiddled with her pearls and looked a bit confused. "Better get you something to eat," she said. "Is mushroom soup all right?" And I grinned at her again and said, "Everything's all right now, Mrs Swanley." Then she asked why the sleeves of my pyjamas were wet and I giggled hysterically and said, "Because I've been to the loo, of course."

The loo. It's just so FUNNY.

But this isn't, Guy. I've been thinking a lot about what you said, about telling your d– Oops. Annabelle gets it wrong again. I mean Tom, Tom, the Woodham's son. I think I will call him Tomdad, actually. I like that. It's sweet. He *has* been a dad to you, hasn't he, Guy? That's what I wanted to say, really. He has looked after you all these years. Just like a true and proper father. And if you really are my brother and Tomdad doesn't know, then that's two people he's lost, isn't it? His wife, and now his almost-son. I feel sorry for him, Guy. I think you should, too. Because he's not as bad as you thought he was, is he? You know that's right because of Sharon. Your Tomdad needed bereavement counselling and you didn't even know it. He was putting on a big brave face all the time. Trying to be strong. For you. I bet.

And then there is *my* nice daddy, of course. Frankdad. BADDAD. Bad because he abandoned you, Guy. Let you grow up with another man. Didn't even call you to tell you the truth when your lovely Mary Mary died.

But it doesn't matter now. Not any more. Everything is to a purpose, remember?

Trust me, Guy. I did tell you you could. I know exactly what I have to do. Mum and the Universe have shown me the way. All I need is a brick and the hammer.

I still love you, Grrr, half-brother or not.

Your silly little Annabelle

PS You have his eyes.

A FUNNY THING HAPPENED ON THE WAY TO THE TOILET . . .

Dear Annabelle,

Or rather in it . . . you've found the locket, haven't you? Well, what's so wonderful about it that it turned your grim day into a wacky one? You could have TOLD me. Were our pictures in it? You know, Alexander and Hermione?

I hope you're feeling better now. You sounded re-fizzed, anyway. What have you been taking? Your message sounded like you'd flipped.

But – WHY didn't you let your Dad tell you whatever he was going to say? I want to know. Tell him Guy wants to know. I'll listen even if you won't. It's about him and my Mum, isn't it? And about me. He was going to actually TELL you. And you stopped him! How could you? You're not taking my fragile nervous system into account. Make sure you get it out of him at the very next opportunity.

I was in the library at lunchtime today, hiding from Jess. She's like a one-girl pack of hounds. I thought I was safe there, surfing the net, but then I looked up and she was coming in the door. Luckily I saw her first, so I nipped behind the carousel of videos and pretended to be studying them carefully. And while I was waiting for her to lose the scent and go out, I noticed what was two centimetres from my nose.

The Winter's Tale.

I looked at it, and it looked back at me. So I've brought it home to watch.

I keep thinking of them at Stratford, watching *The Winter's Tale* of all plays. A pregnant woman and two men. Jealousy. Suspicion. How could they sit there and pretend to be enjoying themselves?

Did watching it MAKE something happen?

I'm going downstairs right now to watch it. Tomdad's out late tonight, visiting some client in Oxford. If you're in town, look out for him. You'll easily recognize him because he looks nothing like me.

As for your Mum's theory of everything in the Universe having a purpose, then what was the purpose of my Mum dying? How does that fit? Ask your Mum when she comes home. Because if she's got an answer that makes sense, I'd really like to hear it.

Halfwit halfbro

YOUR DINNER'S IN THE DOG

Dear Guy,

I hope you are having a lovely evening. I expect by now you have kicked off your trainers, flopped out on the sofa with a can of Tomdad's beer and put the video on. *The Winter's Tale*. Hmm. Can't say I fancy it. Sounds a bit *stuffy* to me, LIKE YOU.

Know what? I think I will have a lazy night, too. I think I will tear up my homework from two days ago, flush it down the perfectly-working loo, go to my wardrobe, put on my prettiest dress and my antique silver locket, then go and take my dog for a walk. And while I am wandering the outskirts of Oxford with my BEST FRIEND by my side, I will think about things. Lots of things. And the first thing I will think about is this: I wonder where the Woodhams keep their telephone? Can it be in the attic, perhaps? Or the deep freezer? Or up the chimney? Or even down the garden where the fairies roam? Surely it can't be in a *normal* place like the hall or the lounge or the kitchen or a bedroom because someone would have ANSWERED it. I wonder why after three attempts to ring my handsome, long-lost brother, who says he is having a night in with Will, all I get is: *I'm sorry, we're not available right now, but if you'd like to leave your name and number . . .*

I wonder why the word JESS keeps coming into my mind?

Oh well, as long as you're enjoying yourself, it doesn't really matter about little sis, does it? I mean, I wouldn't want to disturb your fragile nervous system by actually *talking* to you, mouth to mouth. Some grotty Shakespearean drama is much more important. I do understand that you wouldn't want to know that my dad – your dad – couldn't be bothered to come home tonight because he was going into town to meet an important visitor. Now, I wonder who *that* could be? Gosh, I'm sure I remember someone saying that a certain other important person would be arriving in Oxford tonight . . .

Oh puh, and I did so want to ask our father, who is not in heaven and is never going near it, something at tea-time as well. Now how did it go? Oh yes, I remember: Daddy, darling, Guy would like to know exactly when you DID IT with his mum. Shall we have oven chips, tonight?

Go to a dark place and bury yourself.

Hermione

ONE SORRY FOR EVERY STAR IN THE UNIVERSE . . . AND BEYOND

Guy. I'm sorry.

I'm really, really sorry.

Don't hate me. Forgive me. Please. Say what you like, all the horrible things you want to. I deserve it. I was wicked. I don't know what's the matter with me. I just feel so . . . horribly strange. And lonely too. You did say I could call you if I felt like this. That's why I rang. I needed to talk, to hear your voice. I just want to know you're real, that's all.

I know you wouldn't deliberately ignore my calls. I know there is a proper explanation and everything. You might not believe me because you probably think I'm the most hurtful person in the whole Universe right now, but one of the reasons I was ringing you up was to say there might have been one purpose, one good thing about your mum dying: it brought us together, didn't it?

And now it has probably driven us apart.

I am truly sorry. Hug me in your thoughts,
Miserabelle x

GOT IT STRAIGHT FROM WILL

Dear Annabelle,

I'm sorry too. I mean that I didn't answer the phone. The third time I did answer, but you'd already gone. Just call me Woodlouse. I promise to pick up next time. If you still want to phone that is.

But first, read this. You might not want to phone afterwards. You might not ever want to talk to me again. A, I think I've got it wrong – about me being Franklin's son, I mean. What if we're still brother and sister, but not the way we thought? Can you start to get your head round that? I'm not sure I can.

Before you start tearing your hair out and stuff, listen to this. I knew there must be something in *The Winter's Tale*, and there is. I watched it really closely last night. It doesn't all fit, but an awful lot does. I should have twigged it ages ago when we were reading the play in class, but I must have dozed off for some of the time. Watching it now, it's so obvious.

Annabelle – I thought the baby my Mum was about

to have in that Stratford photo was ME. But supposing it wasn't? Supposing it was –

No, read this first.

Listen, I'm going to tell you the story. Think about it. Let it really sink in. It took me one video and about a month's worth of lessons before I could sort out this plot, so if you can get it from this five-minute version you must be a genius.

OK. Once upon a time, there was a king (nothing to do with your Dad, OK? Don't get confused. Think of him as MY Dad, Tomdad) whose wife was called Hermione. They already had a son, and now Hermione was nine months pregnant. The king's best friend, who he'd known for ages, had been staying with them for the whole nine months and was about to go home.

You can guess what happened. Besides, I've already told you. One day the king looked at Hermione and his friend together and he thought: What if that baby's not mine? What if Hermione's been unfaithful? What if it's HIS? The thought took him over. He was so raving jealous that he even plotted to kill his friend, but the friend cleared off just in time.

Now the king (Tomdad, remember) was even more angry. There was only one person to take it out on. Hermione. So he insulted her and accused her of treason and got her thrown into jail. And there she had her baby daughter.

DAUGHTER.

But the king wasn't finished yet. He got one of his lords to take the baby girl, Perdita, to a far distant country and leave her on the seashore. But the baby didn't die,even though the poor bloke who took her there got eaten by a bear. She was rescued and grew up as a shepherd's daughter and much later came back to the king, her father.

But meanwhile Hermione died . . . The king was grief-stricken. Because he'd sent messengers to the Oracle (that seems to be some sort of Greek-God-Agony-Uncle) and what the Oracle said was that HE'D GOT IT ALL WRONG. Hermione hadn't been unfaithful. He needn't have been jealous. Perdita really was his daughter.

PERDITA REALLY WAS HIS OWN DAUGHTER.

This can't ALL be coincidence, can it? If you're not convinced, go back and read it again, only this time change the names. King = Tom Woodham, my Tomdad. Hermione = my Mum. Best Friend = Dr Franklinstein Murrayfield King. Oh, and Perdita = you. Don't forget that bit. Ask Franklin about it. Ask him why your middle name isn't Perdita. That ought to shake him up a bit.

And by the way, before you change your mind. I love you too. In a brotherly way.

Guy
xxx

BISCUITS AND BYE BYES

Dear Guy,

Thank you very much for that story about *The Winter's Tale*. Funnily enough, I've always liked sheep. I'm afraid it's awkward to talk right now because three policemen are floating round the house. One of them keeps popping his head round the door – just to see what I'm up to, I suppose. You will have to imagine me mailing in a whisper. They turned up half an hour ago, wanting to speak to Frankdad again. I said he had gone to meet a friend. One of them frowned and looked at his watch. He said, "Do you mind if we come in and wait for him, Miss King?" I said, Yes, I did mind, actually, as I was all on my own and not allowed to let strange men into the house – when Mrs Swanley came out of the lounge and said, "Hello, constable. I'm Eleanor Swanley. I live next door. Is everything all right? Should I put the kettle on, Annabelle?" The "constable" flashed his ID. "Detective Inspector actually, madam. Two sugars and a drop of milk for me, please." He looked at me hard. "It's not wise to lie to the police, Miss King."

I had to grit my teeth and try not to stamp. "She was only 'popping in' for *five minutes,*" I growled. "Long enough to make us a brew," he said.

As it happens, I was the one who made the

"brew". While I was waiting for their tea to *stew*, the same policeman came into the kitchen. He told me his name was DI Simon. I told him mine was AH King. We had a polite little chuckle at that. He spread some pictures out on the worktop. Some old Egg-whippity-type of things, photographed in a long glass cabinet. He said, "Do you like jewellery, Miss King?" I squeezed his tea bag and made it break. He shoved a picture under my nose. "You wouldn't have seen anything like that around, would you?"

So I looked at his picture and said we'd done this day trip to the Ashmolean Museum once and there might have been some things like that in there but I wasn't really sure because History wasn't my best subject but Mary Jane would definitely know. Simon stirred his tea and made the little leaves swirl. "Who's Mary Jane?" he asked, lifting the lid off the biscuit barrel.

Guy, my heart was REALLY thumping; you'll find out why in a minute.

"She's the woman I call my mother, " I said. He took a fig roll and looked a bit puzzled. I smiled, had a bourbon and put the lid on the biscuits again. Then he saw the hammer and brick on the table. "Planning a robbery, are you?" he sniffed. I gave him an innocent smile. "No,it's for . . . the walnuts," I said. Before he could ask I grabbed one from the nut bowl, put it on the brick and whomped it with the hammer. "My dog likes walnuts – and our nutcrackers aren't working. Is it all right if I go and type an e-mail on our computer now, please?"

He flicked a bit of walnut shell off his jacket, gave me a sort of detectivey look and wanted to know who it was I was mailing. "My Guy," I said. "He's sort of my boyfriend but more like a brother to me really, I suppose." (I nearly started crying then and had to look away.) "He lives in Herefordshire. We mail each other all the time. I'm helping him with a homework assignment. We're doing Shakespeare. *The Winter's Tale*. Do you know that one? It's all about this king and a shepherd girl. Someone gets eaten by a bear."

Just then there was a noise from the dining-room. Me and Simon glanced at the door. It sounded like his friends were poking around in the chimney. Simon ran his tongue very slowly round his mouth. He stuffed his pictures into a folder. "These items are very valuable," he said. "Some are worth several thousands of pounds. They've gone missing from the University Archaeology Department. If you saw anything like that you would inform us, wouldn't you, Miss King?" Hmph. I was about to explain that it's nothing to do with me really, I just happen to live here with these two people but actually I'm no relation at all, when he cocked his head and this smug little smile rolled over his face. He pointed an accusing finger. "Why is your blouse buttoned up to the neck?" "Why shouldn't it be?" I said, getting a bit prickly. "It looks a little *tight* at the collar," he said. "You wouldn't be concealing anything, would you, Miss King? Like a piece of *jewellery*, for instance?"

I got huffy, then, cos I haven't shown my neck to anyone in ages. "I've got a bruise," I blushed. "A love bite, if you must know." He pinched his nose. I could tell he didn't believe me. So I undid my top two buttons and showed him exactly what Stinkler had done. He took a quick look and his mouth sort of crunkled down at the edges. "Yes, well, thanks for the tea," he grunted and slid the cup across the worktop. I caught it and started to rinse it out. But as soon as he had gone I dried my hands, rummaged about in the bottom of the biscuit tin, found what he was *really* looking for, slipped it round my neck and did my blouse back up.

And now I will have to be off, because if they come in and read that they will take me away. In a minute I am going to trot downstairs and ask, pretty please, can I go and walk Ginger? I know they'll say yes because they trust me now. They have put the football on and are going to wait "as long as it takes" for "my father" to come home. Huh. They'll have a pretty long wait.

I have fed Rocket and done the washing-up. Mrs Swanley is looking after the Flatfoots. If a Dr F King should call later in a mad panic, will you please tell him Ginger is safe with me. I've decided we are going for a long walk tonight. We might be out some time. I need to get my head round things as you say. Namely:

* I hate that man I've always thought was my dad.
* My real dad doesn't even know I'm his daughter. (Could you give him the phone number for that Oracle thingy?)
* If I hadn't just found out my true identity, I would now be the daughter of a Wanted Woman.
* The only boy I've ever loved just happens to be my brother.
* My mum is dead.

I wish my parents, whoever they are, had left me on a distant seashore at birth.

But I did get A* for my poem, this week. Ms Spence says it's going on our website (groan). I hope you are proud of me. I am of you.

Goodbye, Guy. Think of me sometimes. Just off to walk Ginger.

Your loving Perdy. xxx

PLEASE PHONE

Annabelle, why haven't you phoned? I waited and waited.

Guy

IS THERE ANYBODY THERE?

Annabelle,

Perdita means lost. Did I tell you? You're not lost, are you? Just gone out for a walk The policeman told me when I finally phoned. But why did you end your message like that? Where are you going?

Police – again? Have you found out why they're interested in that locket – is it stolen, then? They don't think it could be your mum who hid it, do they?

Are you there? Are you frightened? Why aren't you phoning or mailing? And where's Franklin? He's gone out to meet my dad, I know he has. What are they up to?

Please don't be lost. Its all my fault. Come back. Mail me. Phone. I'll do anything.

Where *are* you?
Guy xxx

A N-N-NIGHT TO REMEMBER

Dear Annabelle,

This feels so weird. I mean, all this time, I've been e-mailing you not really knowing what you look like part from that cheeky grin in the netball pic, a bit blurry) or what you sound like. Now I do know who's at the other end. I've seen you. I've talked to you. I've even hugged you. I know who I'm writing to. And I know what your face will look like when you read this.

You are there, aren't you? I didn't dream it all?

It felt like dreaming when the doorbell rang and I found you on my front doorstep. And when you sort of fell in through the doorway like a sleepwalker. That taxi-driver who'd brought you all that way looked a bit dubious about leaving you with me. Fair enough, I suppose. It was past midnight and it must have seemed weird to dump you on some strange boy who was too shell-shocked even to say Hello. And it took me so long to fetch my savings and Dad's secret hoard and then count out all those coins that I hardly even looked at you, at first. But I was so relieved you were safe. I thought you'd gone completely mad and had set off for France or Scotland or somewhere, hitch-hiking. And it would all have been my fault.

I don't know what our Dads expected to find when they burst in like that. And then everyone was talking at once and it all got a bit confused. But the one thing that wasn't confused was getting our own Dads back. I'd got that utterly, completely, fantastically wrong and you must think I'm completely off my head. I'm really sorry. Sorry x a hundred. But there's one thing I'm not sorry about. That it brought you here.

Anyway, n-n-now you kn-kn-kn-know what I sound like and why I n-n-never phoned you when you asked me to. I kn-kn-know I should have told you, especially when you came clean about being in Year N-n-n-nine. But I didn't have the guts. I thought you'd n-n-never want to speak to me again. I was about to tell you about it when our Dads crashed in. So here it is.

I haven't always stammered. I used to when I was very small and then I had speech therapy and got over it. Then, when my Mum died, it came back. Badly. I'm supposed to have therapy again, only I'm always finding excuses not to go. I don't always stammer. Only when I'm upset or nervous – in other words, all the times when I most don't want to stammer. That's why I hate reading aloud in class and French orals and things like that. Mark calls me G-G-Guy the G-G-Glbberer, even though it's only N sounds I get stuck on. I don't know what happens. I know what I want to say and then it sort of gets stuck in the roof of my mouth and won't come out. It's awful when people look away, embarrassed (how do they think *I* feel?) or say the N word for me, as if I'm an idiot. You didn't do either of those things and I was glad.

So of course I stammered like mad when you turned up, specially as my dad had just phoned and said, "Annabelle's on her way." I couldn't have been more amazed if he'd said the Queen of Sheba was dropping in. You were here five minutes later, but that gave me five minutes to work up to a full-scale tongue-jam. I hoped you'd think I was the strong, silent type, but really you must have thought I was mental, and I wouldn't have blamed you if you'd called your taxi-driver back and told him to take you straight home again. I was getting better though, wasn't I, while we were talking? Perhaps if I saw you often enough I'd stop doing it altogether.

Anyway, that's it. I just wanted to explain.

Are you OK now? I really, really hope so. When I phoned the second time and that policeman put MY DAD on the line (I thought my brain had short-circuited or something!) and then YOUR DAD took over, sounding completely frantic, I felt like a murderer – it was all my fault you'd run away. If you've told your Dad why – all the things I made you believe, because I believed them myself – he'll never forgive me, let alone want you to see me again.

At least they've promised to tell us everything now. My Dad's going to tell me tonight I'll e-mail you about it. I could phone, but I've got used to e-mailing and I like it and don't want to stop. So I'm going to e-mail AND phone.

And . . . Annabelle, I've been to your school website and read your *My Guy* poem. Do you really mean it? Or rather, DID you mean it? And if so, do you still mean it? In spite of knowing how I talk, and everything?

Because – I suppose we were too confused to take it in properly at the time, but now it's finally got through to my brain – we're NOT brother and sister, we're not related at all, not even half-related. So if we want to meet again (I mean in a more normal way than hi-jacking taxi-drivers in the middle of the night, I mean GOING OUT), we can.

I want to. Do you?

Guy, your n-n-n-not-brother
xxxxxxxxx

SHE'S BACK!

Dear Hero,

It's me! I'm here. Your favourite apparition. A bit snuffled with a cold (it rains a lot on the Welsh borders, doesn't it?) but almost back to full fizz.

Guess what this is?

:*

A kiss, in Internet speak. I've been meaning to tell you that for weeks. Here's another :* to say thanks for looking after me and another :* to prove I still love you. Anyway, get a load of this: MONSTER NEWS.

SHE WHO MUST BE OBEYED IS BACK!

Yep, she arrived home yesterday, exactly one day early. She was waiting for us when we got home from your house. If I hadn't got one of your Herefordshire colds I would have detected the camelly smell from miles away.

It was weird. We opened the door and there she was, flouncing towards us with Rocket in her arms. "Mary!" Dad spluttered. I thought he was going to pass out. He scratched his head and looked at his watch. "Oh Franklin, do stop frowning," she said. "I caught an earlier flight, that's all." Then she switched her gaze to me and said, "What's the matter, A?"

My mum. She always knows when something's wrong. I couldn't hide a feather up my jumper from her.

I went rushing forward and threw my arms around her. "Steady on, child," she whispered, adjusting her hands so she could hold my head against her shoulder, "you don't want to squash this little chap, do you? It is ours, I take it?" I nodded my head. (Mum loves cats.) "His name's Rocket," I sniffed. "Dad got him for my birthday." She stroked Rocket's head. "Did he now? How thoughtful of him. So where have you two been?" "The Woodhams," Dad said. "It's a long story." I felt Mum nod her head. She gave me a kiss, then handed Rocket over. "Go and lie down for a while," she said. "You look utterly exhausted. I'll come up and see you when I've spoken to your father."

Dad mumbled something under his breath and flung his keys on the telephone table. "Mary," he said, "*you*'re jet-lagged, *I*'ve had a long drive; there's a time and place for this." "Quite right," she replied. "I would suggest the dining-room but it seems to be full of soot. Kitchen. Now." Ooh, bad news. He ought to know better than to mess with Mum.

Guy, they must have argued for *hours*. She barked so loud Ginger flattened his ears and wriggled right underneath my bed. For once, I couldn't bear to listen – me, super snoop, copping out. I climbed into bed with a box of tissues, put my headphones on and played that tape you gave me. They're not bad, are they? The Beatles, I mean. And I easily guessed which song you said should be "ours". I'm mad at you now cos I can't stop singing it! It's *From Me to You*, isn't it? Except it ought to be *From E to You*, really. But it sounds like that when you sing it, doesn't it? And what do you mean, "Did Ginger start to howl, then?" Guy Woodham, I have a beautiful voice. It goes with my lovely n-n-nose, which I haven't washed since you k-kissed it for me . . . (Twice as I recall. Very forward.) And while I'm "waxing lyrical" (one of Dad's favourite phrases), I want to say this . . .

I know you're there
in the ether, all around me
like the comfort of a warm wind
touching my heart

because it's true. And gulp, BIG confession. I WANTED you to read my poem. That's why I told you it was going on our website. I know I pretended to groan and everything, but I was all in a tizz then and not really sure what I was going to do – y'know, when I ran away. If I *had* turned up on a distant seashore or been found curled up in a bus shelter or something (dying of a broken heart), I just wanted you to know . . . y'know, how I felt . . . uh oh, snuffles coming on. Time for a tissue. Or two. Or half a box.

And of course I don't mind about your stammer. Silly old G. It doesn't bother me at all. And I'm not saying that just because you're incredibly gorgeous and a few n-n-n-nuhs would be worth putting up with n-n-now and again. I'm n-n-n-not that kind of girl.

I did wonder, when I flopped out on your sofa, why you were choosing your words so carefully. I thought you just didn't like me at first, especially when you spent about an HOUR in the kitchen making me that cup of drinking chocolate. If you'd never offered me that bana-n-nah-n-nana we might never have said a single word – not that we said that much anyway. Wasn't it weird having all that time alone together and not talking about the Marys or the locket or anything, just looking at one another? If you'd have said. "I can't believe you're here" just one more time I think I would have suggested an echo therapist, not a speech therapist.

Anyway, your stammer did us a favour. As soon as you started I knew right away why you hadn't phoned me.You looked so unhappy, standing there with your head bent low and your lovely fringe curving into your eyes. But when you came to sit beside me and you cried a bit too, I knew it would all be all right in the end. Sorry I made a wet patch on your fleece. (I'm not, really, cos it made you take it off. Phwooaarrr!)

But Guy, you don't *ever* have to be nervous around me again. And do you know what? You didn't stammer once when you used my name or when you stood up for me when the Dad Patrol burst in. "You're NOT going to hurt her!" Ooh, what a yunk! I thought you were going to clobber my dad. He didn't half look small. Talking of which. That Mark is horrible for calling you Guy the Gibberer. He'll be Mark the Mustard Seed (smallest "M" thing I could think of) when I see him. No one should make fun of you like that. I could understand it if you'd been the sort of boy who picks his nose and makes pyramids with the balls of snot. Then again, I have still to receive your list of disgusting habits. So I will reserve my final judgement for now and move on swiftly to other matters . . .

After a while Mum came up to my room with a tray of toasted tea-cakes and a glass of warm milk. We had a big, BIG talk. A real girly job. We nattered about all the normal stuff first, mainly how her dig had gone, and all about school and my SATS tests (yawn).

She wasn't too impressed about Tracey getting the part of Cleo. "Whatever could Ms Spence be thinking?" she said. "Dreadful bit of casting. She's right out of character. Hardly a ravishing beauty, is she?" Which cheered me up LOADS. "You mean, *I*'m a ravishing beauty?" I asked. She stuck out her chin and said, "Somebody thinks so," and pushed my jama collar aside.

She went *ballistic* when she saw Stinkler's lovebite, and dubble ballistic when I told her why. I think she thought you'd done it at first. "Mu-um," I sighed. "Guy thought he was my brother, then; he'd hardly give me a lovebite, would he?" She gritted her teeth at that. "Oh yes," she said. "I've heard all about Master Woodharn's theories. He's got a dafter imagination than you have. It's a good job he isn't here right now, I'd have a word or two to say to that young man." I got a bit stroppy then and blew my nose loudly. "Well, it's all Dad's fault for having a picture of . . . y'know, Mrs Woodham, in his wallet." At least that made her hoot with laughter. "Mrs Woodham?" she repeated. "She wouldn't like that. Far too formal for Mary." Then she turned all serious again and gave me a gentle prod in the shoulder. "We'll talk about that little peck later, madam. And while we're on the subject of major misdoings, it wasn't your father asked you to get into a taxi in the middle of the night and go haring up to the Welsh border, was it?" I lowered my gaze and felt a bit ashamed. "It was only half-past ten," I pouted. But she wouldn't let me off. "It was a reckless and silly thing to do," she said. "For goodness' sake, A, what if something terrible had happened?" Then she stroked my hair and I had a good weep and we hugged each other for absolutely ages.

Oh yes, while I'm thinking about it, I promised I'd tell you how I escaped and what happened after I'd left the house, didn't I? Getting out was mega-easy. First I walked Ginger twice round the block, checking every time he stopped to piddle that DI Simon wasn't following me. When I was sure I was all alone, I nipped through the gap in Mrs Swanley's hedge, into our back garden, shut Ginger in the shed – and did a runner.

Five minutes' walk from where we live there's this

little taxi place. Dad has a special arrangement with them. If Mum's away and he's at work, I'm supposed to get a taxi home (from Laura's or my drama group and stuff). Dad pops round the next day and pays the fare. So I just waltzed in and said, "I'd like a taxi, please." And Jeetpal, who drives me to lots of places, folded up his paper and said, "Sure, let's go." We were in the cab when he asked where to. "47 Llanwarne Rise," I replied. (I'd found you in Dad's address book by then.) "You have to go out towards the main A40. West – no, north-west, I think." Jeetpal tugged his earring. "Llanwarne Rise?" he asked. "Is it on one of the new estates?"

That was a scary moment. I bit my lip and said, dead calmly, "No . . . it's in Herefordshire." The taxi screeched to a halt. Jeetpal looked over his shoulder. "You're kidding me, yeah?" I shook my head. "I'm staying with one of my relations," I said. "I want to get there before midnight if possible." And Jeetpal fell for it – until we reached the outskirts of Hereford, that is, when we screeched to a halt in the middle of a bridge.

Back home, Dad had sussed it out. He'd told the police to check the taxi place and they called Jeetpal on the radio. Jeetpal was going to turn back at first, but by then we were only a few miles from your house and Dad told the police he would fetch me back from there himself. So you see, you didn't have to pay the fare, really. But I was proud of you all the same. I suppose Jeetpal was hardly going to refuse the money – even if it was all twenty pence pieces. Did you give him a tip?

When I told Mum this she frowned a bit and said she was going to have "a word" with that taxi firm. Better than that, she's going to "bend a few ears" at the police station tomorrow. She wasn't very pleased about them coming in "uninvited" and snooping round the house. "Reasonable grounds for suspicion," she rumbled. "They didn't have reasonable grounds for coffee! Worrying a defenceless fourteen-year-old with some trumped-up garbage about international jewellery heists. It's NOT ON." (Cor, I bet they'll wish they hadn't rummaged through her knicker drawer. If I was DI Simon I think I'd lock myself away in a nice tight cell tomorrow morning.)

This got us on to the locket, of course. If you thought you were ready to dissolve into a puddle when your dad was ranting, "OF COURSE SHE'S NOT YOUR SISTER, YOU THUNDERING GREAT LEMON!" (v. unfair, I thought) you could have fried an egg on my dainty cheeks when Mum put her hand in her cardigan pocket, pulled out the locket and laid it on the duvet. "I believe your father confiscated this at the Woodhams? I expect you'd like me to explain all about it?" Honestly, I didn't know where to look. "Did you steal it?" I whispered.

"How long will you get?" She pinched my nose and waggled it about. "Annabelle, don't be ridiculous," she tutted. "This locket *belongs* to me; it's been in the family for generations." I looked up slowly. "You mean . . . I've got Egyptian ancestors?" I seriously, SERIOUSLY thought for one moment she was going to tell me that Queen Cleopatra was my ancient grannie. Instead, she rolled her eyes and said: "Haven't I taught you anything, child? Does it look like it's come from the middle of a pyramid? It's Victorian. It belonged to my mother and her mother before that. It's an heirloom. Here, let me see it on."

She popped it round my neck. It felt good to be wearing it again, as if it was somehow protecting me. "But Mum," I said, "if it's just an heirloom, why was Dad so mad when we found it?" She moved the chain aside and inspected my mole. "Mixture of anger and embarrassment," she said. "He wasn't expecting it to be beneath the boards, and you weren't supposed to see it – not until your eighteenth birthday, anyway. It was intended to be a surprise gift – as it was for my coming of age. I discovered that loose board ages ago.Whenever I'm away I always hide the locket there, purely because your father has never got around to installing the security devices I've so often begged him to. Just my luck to have that roly poly pudding (Jupiter, she meant) breach my defences and blow the gaff. Outwitted by a rodent. Whatever next?"

My mole, that was next. "Does that thing itch?" she asked. I told her it didn't and it hadn't grown a hair since Dr Keelan saw it and to please not change the subject. "But why did the police come and look for it?" I said. She sighed a bit wearily and shook her head. "They didn't; they were after something else. Some months ago, several rare artefacts went missing from the university's Egyptian Studies Department. The culprit was never found. The day before I went to Luxor, two more small items disappeared. Your charming Mr Plod, one clue short of a full crossword, took it into his head that this had all the markings of an inside job and decided I was his prime suspect."

Well, I nearly hit the roof! "How could ANYONE think you were a robber?"

She lifted an eyebrow and gave me a "well, you just did" sort of look. I blushed and fiddled with a tissue. "But didn't Dad tell them how honest you are? He couldn't believe you'd steal anything?" She ran a finger under her chin. "He didn't, he was much more inventive than that. He knew how much those artefacts meant to me and how upset I was when they were lost, so he came to the rather bizarre conclusion that I might have removed the latest items from our departmental archives and hidden them here for safekeeping." I made a screwy face. "Is that why he had his head up the chimney? He was looking for all your hiding-places?" "Apparently," Mum muttered, wincing a bit. "He claims that my secrecy about the locket gave him every reason to act like he did." "He's barmy," I said. Mum nodded in agreement. "The problem was, once he'd got the notion into his head, things just went from bad to worse. He then began to think, How would it look if the police searched the house and THEY turned up the missing items? Or worse, what if we were burgled and the police discovered that the robbers had made off with a lovely little haul of Egyptian swag? That got him into a right old tizz." I groaned and said, "Why didn't he just ring your dig and ask?!" "Ooh no,"Mum said, pretending to frown. "That would have been far too dangerous." She leaned forward and whispered, "What if the phones were being tapped?" I slapped my hand across my face. "Oh, it gets better than that," she laughed. "Because he knew the house was so vulnerable to a break-in, he then proceeded – after ten years of fruitless nagging – to install some security devices." I groaned again and told her how Rocket had set off the infra-red thingy. "Hmm. Well, good for Rocket," Mum said. "But not so good for your father. While helping the police with their silly inquiries, he managed to drop a receipt on the floor of their interview room – detailing all his security purchases. He must have looked as guilty as a kitten. Your father's a brilliant man, Annabelle, but when he's confronted by figures of authority or any suggestion of lawlessness he seems to just sag at the knees of reason. It didn't help when you disappeared with the locket." "Well, why was he hiding it from me?" I barked. "I've told you," she repeated quietly. "You weren't supposed to see it yet. He knew you'd turn the house upside-down looking for it. The cistern was hardly the best of places to hide an expensive antique, but I suppose I should at least give him credit for trying."

Well, I didn't know what to say for a bit. I just caressed the locket a while and was grateful I hadn't gone through with my plans about the hammer and the brick. "I nearly smashed it once," I confessed. Mum reeled back "Good Lord, child. Whatever for?" I shrugged and turned redder than a ripe tomato. "Let me guess," she said. "You thought it was all mixed up with your father and . . . Mrs Woodham?" I shook my head. "I thought it was a gift from your Arab lover first." She roared with laughter at that. "Oh dear," she said, rubbing my hand. "You have had a bit of a trial, haven't you?" I gave a little nod – and then I got really tight inside (cos you know what's coming next).

I said. "Mum, you know you said about Dad and Guy's mum? Why *has* he got a photo of her in his wallet?" She went quiet and fussed with the tea tray a moment. "No," she said suddenly, slapping her thigh, "your father got himself into this mess. I think he should be the one to explain about Mary."

"Aw, Mum!" I protested. But she wouldn't give in. All she would say was, "A, it was a long, long time ago. Let's just leave it at that, shall we?"

And I thought that was going to be the end of our talk But in a way, it was just the beginning. I was blowing my nose when Rocket sneaked in through the door, jumped on my bed and sat up, staring – just like he'd done in my dream. This awful shiver ran across my shoulders and I heard myself saying, "Mum, I had a funny dream last week – you were in it; you were out in the desert." "What's so funny about that?"she said. "I practically live in the desert." I looked straight at her. "You had a child in your arms. A little baby boy. He had dark hair. You were giving him to me . . ."

Guy, her face turned straight to stone.

"Mum?" I said. "Mum, what's the matter?" I'd never ever seen her like that before. "Oh God," she said, grasping for the duvet. "How could you know? How could you possibly know?" I wriggled out of bed and threw my arms around her. "What?" I said. "What did I know? It was just a dream, Mum. Please, what's the matter?" "Oh God," she said again, covering her eyes. "I'm so, so sorry. I should have told you years ago. Oh, Annabelle. Forgive me. I'm sorry." And I was frightened then because I knew that something terrible had happened and I was desperate to make it right for her. "What about?" I gulped. "Tell me. Please. You are my real mum, aren't you . . . Mum?" She half-laughed, half-cried and put a palm on my cheek. "I'm so grateful for you," she sobbed. "Whatever would I do without you? I had a miscarriage, A, before you were born. You should have had an elder brother. We were going to call him Alexander . . ."

Guy, I thought the world would explode all around me, but the door just opened and Dad came in. He looked at Mum, sat down quietly on the end of the bed, gathered her slowly into his arms and rocked her like the son she never had.

I'm sorry, I will have to log off for a bit. It was so, so awful and writing about it is making me weepy. Please be patient. Now is not a good time to ask Dad things. But if you know anything, will you tell me, please?

I miss you (already!),
Your soggy Annabawl
:* :* :*

STRAIGHT TALKING AT THE WOODHAMS

Dear Annabelle,

My Dad told me about your lost brother, too. I wasn't sure whether to say anything in case you didn't know.

But Woodham Father and Son have a new policy of telling things straight, now, and that's obviously happening in your house too. Dad and I had a long talk tonight. At last, after weeks of stepping round each other like boxers sizing up their opponents. I started it in my usual clodhopping way by saying, "You're going to tell me everything now, aren't you, Dad? Because if not, I'll get it from Franklin, via Annabelle."

He looked a bit sad. "No, you don't have to do that," he said. "Though there's been a fair bit of that going on, hasn't there? I'll tell you what you want to know. It's time I did. You can ask me anything and I'll answer. But first," he said ominously, "I've got to tell you, in case you haven't already worked it out for yourself – you've been pretty irresponsible, Guy. Telling that poor little girl all that twaddle about *The Winter's Tale* and lost babies and muddled parents and nearly sending her off her head –"

I nearly exploded. "POOR LITTLE GIRL?" I burst out. "Are you talking about *Annabelle*? You saw her, didn't you? She's nearly as tall as I am and she's n-n -n -"

I NEVER stammer with Dad. NEVER. Only when there are other people about.

He just looked at me. Then he said, very quietly, "I see." And I said, "Oh yeah? WHAT do you see?" He said, "I see that your mother really started something when she suggested you and Annabelle might get in touch."

I was gobsmacked. (Sorry, Mum. A, my mum always hated that word. But for this I can't think of a better one.) "MUM suggested it?" I blurted. "Oh yes," Dad said. "It was Mum's idea, to start with. When she wrote to Franklin and Jane." "She wrote to them? When?"

So he told me. Mum wrote all sorts of letters, the last few weeks, to be posted on. There was one she wrote to me. It's even longer than one of yours, and I'll always keep it, but it's too private to show even to you. Anyway, among these letters there was one addressed to your Mum and Dad. It was sealed, so Dad didn't read it But then Franklin told him on the phone that Mum had said how nice it would be if you and I met one day.

She was absolutely right. It is. Thank you, Mum.

Next, I asked him (Straight Talking Policy in action): "Annabelle's Dad loved Mum, didn't he? Don't you mind? I thought –"

He gave me what Mum used to call A LOOK. "Yes, I know what you thought," he said. "You did quite a lot of thinking, most of it half-witted. It's true, they were more than good friends, before your Mum and I got together. But you got it into your head that he was your father, didn't you? Did you seriously believe that?" "Well – yes,yes, I did," I confessed. "I mean, he seemed so interested in me, and everyone always says I look like Mum but never like you, and it all seemed to fit –"

"Guy," he said, with a sort of sad smile. "Yes, you do look like her. Sometimes it breaks my heart. Especially that expression – that one there." Of course I tried to catch it,but I haven't a clue what was on my face just then. Probably total gobsmacked stupidity, same as usual, only that would be insulting to Mum. "But haven't you ever looked at your feet?" Dad said.

I looked at them. Dad laughed. "Not with trainers and socks on," he goes. "Take them off and look at your feet." I gave him A LOOK then, but I took my shoes and socks off and so did he. "Look at those feet," he said, "all four of them, and now tell me I'm not your father. Haven't you ever noticed before?"

So I looked at all those feet. Weird things, aren't they, feet, when you really look at them? But Dad's right. We've got the same feet. Identical, except Dad's are hairier. Even the same-shaped toenails on all our toes. I don't know what your feet are like, Annabelle, but our four are sort of long and thin (size ten in my case, flipping great onkeybats Mum used to call them (and don't ask me where onkeybats comes from, cos I haven't a clue) with long big toes and all the others sort of tapering. They're rather elegant feet, now I think about it. I know what Mark's feet are like and they're squared-off at the toes. I've noticed that because he gets on far better with his walking boots than I do. I'm always getting rubbed toe places.

So my feet aren't designed for walking boots but they do prove I'm my own Dad's son. And I'm pleased, because I'd rather have him than Franklin, and anyway Franklin's yours. Have a look at Franklin's onkeybats and I bet his aren't the same. I've got Woodham feet, not King feet. (You've got A King feet. Hah!)

So there's Dad and me staring at our feet, the Woodham Foot Appreciation Society, with all these shoes and socks all over the carpet. "You're my son all right, Guy," he said. "Thank God. You're all I've got, now."

I felt a bit choked up. I said, "Sorry, Dad. About all that stupid stuff. Cos I don't want any other Dad." "Do you mean that?" he said, and I said Yes, honest. Then he told me about the four of them at York, how they met. And all about your Dad and my Mum . . .

Mary Mary and Mary Jane had been friends since the very first day, they had rooms next to each other, and Franklin and Tom were mates too. My Mum and your Dad started going out as soon as they met in the drama society, and when it was all over, they stayed friends. All four of them were in halls of residence for the first year, but had to find their own flats after that. When our Mums were looking for a place, this house came up, big enough for four, and they decided to ask our Dads to share with them. So that was how my Mum and my Dad met each other – in a way, Franklin introduced them! And it was also how YOUR Mum and Dad met each other – my Mum introduced yours to Franklin. So if it hadn't been for your Dad, I wouldn't be here, and if it hadn't been for my Mum, YOU wouldn't have existed. Weird or what?

Dad says they were the happiest days of his life, sharing that house in York. "Not counting when you came along," he said as a quick afterthought. "So how did you all lose touch then?" I asked. "If you were all such good friends,and all so happily paired off?" He got sad again then. And that's when he told me about Alexander.

What happened was this. A couple of years after they left York, my Mum got pregnant with me. Soon after, your Mum got pregnant too, with Alexander. But I arrived, bang on time, all kicking and healthy and – well, you know what happened to Alexander. It was awful, Dad said. Your Mum and Dad came round to visit a couple of times but none of them could bear it. I reminded your parents of the baby they hadn't got, and my parents didn't feel it was right to be happy and didn't know what to say to them. Once, Franklin held me. He asked if he could have me to hold, just for a minute, and he cuddled me. And my Dad just knew he was thinking of his own son, and that if he'd married my Mum he might have been holding his own baby. Dad said, all three of them stared at Franklin holding me and closing his eyes in a sort of trance, not wanting to give me back, and Dad knew they were all thinking the same thing. Your Mum didn't hold me. They asked if she wanted to, but she went choky and uptight and told Franklin she wanted to go home. And that was the last time they ever met, all four of them together.

It's so weird, Annabelle, imagining all this. There am I in the middle of it, that baby.

And even after you were born, they never got round to meeting each other again. Even the Christmas cards fizzled out after a while.

And A, it really was confession time, because my Dad told me he's always been a bit jealous of Franklin. He said, "Franklin was always better-looking than I am, and miles cleverer, and funnier, and far more successful. I mean, look at him now. Lecturer in Classics, big house in Oxford, articles published in journals. And what am I? A boring bog-standard accountant with receding hair, living in an ordinary semi. Guy, to be honest, I often wondered if Mary thought she'd have done better to stick to him, after all."

What happened next still does my head in. I started to say, "No, Dad, of course she didn't –" when his face sort of crumpled up and his mouth twisted and his shoulders heaved, and next minute he was crying. He stopped even trying to hide it. "I miss her," he kept saying. "I miss her so much, Guy." And then I started too. And we both needed to blow our noses and there weren't any tissues because only Mum would ever have thought of buying any, so Dad dashed to the bathroom and came back with a loo roll and we both sat there blubbing away and snatching bits of bog roll and gulping. Dad put his arm round me and for ages neither of us said anything. And Annabelle, I don't know if this is an awful thing to think, but l did think it – it was almost FUNNY, the two of us sitting there cuddling, bawling away like a couple of babies. Eventually, when we'd got right down to the cardboard tube in the middle, Dad said, all sniffy, "I think that probably did us both a lot of good."

And I tried to say – but I could hardly speak for gulping - "I didn't know, Dad!" What I meant was, I didn't know you cared so much. I thought you'd got over it. But I think Dad understood what I meant. He said, "I know. I've hidden my feelings a bit too well, haven't I?" And I said, "Why?" He said, "Not because I didn't care. NOT because I've got over it. It's not something I'll ever get over, losing Mary." And his voice went wobbly and I thought he was going to start all over again, but he said, "It was because I felt I had to stay in control, for you. You had to feel some things were normal. But I was wrong. I shouldn't have pretended. I should have spent more time talking to you, Guy, and I'm sorry."

So I said, "It's all right, Dad. We're talking now, aren't we?"

And we did.

Then, after a bit, Dad got up and made us both a cup of tea, with fruit cake. When we'd had it I told him I was going to e-mail you. He said, "OK, but why not phone her? I mean, she knows now how self-conscious you are about talking. If it didn't matter yesterday, it's not going to matter today. What's stopping you? You're surely not thinking of my phone bill?" So I told him I'd probably phone as well, but some things are better e-mailed. I said, "I want to tell her all about this. Annabelle and I tell each other everything."

But I'll be on the phone later too. And no, I'm not thinking of his bill.

Guy Red-Nose
:* :* :* :* :*

PS Ninety-nine noisy nuns natter nightly in Nuneaton. Got it in one! Not a single hesitation.

COFFEE SHOP CONFESSIONS

Dear Rudolph,

Thanks for last night's mega-message. Cor, what a lot of romantic goings-on. I never knew parents could be so exciting. I've just had another monster gab with Mum. She told me loads more stuff about Alexander, and York, and your mum, and your dad – she even mentioned his feet! Yuk. Tell you in a minute.

First I want to say I'm not sorry you had a big sob with your dad because it got your feelings in the open, didn't it? See, I told you he cared about your mum. I lick my finger and go "puh" at you. I have to confess I'm impressed with your tear ducts. A WHOLE loo roll? Right down to the tube? Wow, that's my kind of Guy! I'm afraid it doesn't quite beat my best blubbing effort – which was last year when Laura got *The Sound of Music* out on video and we thought it would be boring and ended up sharing half a box of tissues, the end of a kitchen roll, a tea-towel and Ginger's neck by the time they were crooning *Edelweiss*. But it's a scorching effort all the same. Highest new entry in the charts, I'd say.

Sorry it's taken me ages to write back. I was going to log on after breakfast this morning, but then Mum asked did I want to go shopping? Sorry, Guy. You can't turn down an offer to shop! And as I came downstairs, Laura phoned. She wanted to know where I'd been for the past few days and said everyone at school was asking about me and there were rumours going round that I had a rare disease and I said, "Yes, it's called LOVE," and she said I had to spill *right there and then* or she'd die and probably never wake up. After half an hour of Guytalk, Mum got annoyed and rapped, "Annabelle, it is a scientifically-proven fact that holding a telephone receiver to the shell of the ear for more than twenty minutes weakens the cartilage and leaves the lobes susceptible to disintegration the first time a boy tries to nibble them – so if you plan to have interesting times in the back row of the cinema, get off the phone NOW!" I told Laura all that and she giggled and said Mum was totally crackers – but she'd check it out with Gina, just in case!

So, Mum and me trogged round town, arm in arm, on a tour of the charity shops. It was great. I got a spiffy new micro top and a denim bag with a happy-beamy sunflower sewn on the side. "Very sixties," Mum said (whatever that's supposed to mean). Then we went to a hi-fi place and she bought me a personal CD player for my birthday – yes! (My presents from Mum are always late, when she's been away on a dig.) And . . . wait for this . . . then she took me to a really posh jeweller's and had a brand new silver chain fitted to the locket which I now officially own (swank). "Couldn't bear you pestering me about it for the next three and a half years," she said, while we were chatting over a coffee later. She even showed me how to *open* it. "You mean you haven't solved it yet?" she said. "You'll be pleased to know you don't need a hammer. Just hold it like this, press here and . . ." Dink. There it was. In two halves. I couldn't believe it. And guess who was in it? Me and Dad. The two big loves of her life, she said. I sat there gawping for several seconds, not sure I should say what was in my mind – but of course, I did!

I told her that in my dream, Alexander and Hermione had been in the locket. She fingered the rim of her coffee cup and said, "I may not have a picture of Alexander, but I often imagine him in that locket. In case you're wondering, it's not entirely coincidental that Guy shares a middle name with your brother. At York, Mary and I often used to muse over what we would call our children. Alexander was always a mutual favourite."

Spooky, huh? Anyway, she was obviously in a mood to talk about "things", so I went for a biggie: "Why was I called Hermione, Mum? I asked Dad once and he went, 'Oh God.' She tightened her lips into a very thin smile. "That's because you touched a nerve," she said. "He met Mary during a student production of . . . oh, what's the play called?" "*The Winter's Tale*," I muttered. "Ah yes," Mum nodded, "the source of Master Woodham's inspiration. Franklin was always encouraging Mary to play the great Shakespearean heroines, but she had such appalling stage fright that bit parts were all she could really hold down. To keep her spirits up he used to tell her she would always be 'his Hermione' – until you came along, of course."

I frowned at her hard and went a bit bristly. I've still

got a major bag on with Dad and wasn't in the mood to be "his Hermione". Anyway, fancy him replacing your mum with me! Mum guessed what I might be thinking and said, "You're being too hard on him, Annabelle. He loves you to bits; you know that, really. I want you to make it up with him."

No chance! I scowled like mad and told her I hated him. She frowned and tapped my hand. "But Mum," I tutted, "first he named me after his girl-friend and now he's got a picture of her in his wallet. Aren't you jealous?" She leaned forward on her elbows and sipped her coffee. "Under any other circumstances I might have been, yes. But for one thing, I rather liked the name too, and Mary wasn't just "a girlfriend", A. She and your father were very close once. Did you know he took that photo?" That sent a funny little shiver down my spine. Mum saw me twitch, but carried straight on: "It used to stand on the mantelpiece at Caverner Road. She must have taken it with her when we all left." I wrinkled my nose up and said, "You mean he hasn't always had it?" Mum shook her head. "It arrived in a letter shortly after she'd died, a letter explaining all about her illness and hoping he'd forgive her for not sharing the end." "Did he?" I asked (reluctant-ly). Mum paused and looked out at the dreaming spires. "No. He was absolutely devastated. Don't you remember how miserable he was in the middle of last year? Didn't you ever wonder why we cancelled our holiday?" I gulped and started to shake a bit. "You said he was ill," I mumbled. She nodded. "He was; hopelessly depressed. Losing Mary like that was a dreadful shock. I really felt very sorry for him."

Huh. That got me in a right old huff. I wasn't going to forgive him *that* easily. "He still put the photo in his wallet," I griped. "That meant he loved her more than you."

Guy, you will not believe what happened next. She clunked her coffee cup down and said, "Oh Annabelle, you're far too young to understand." WHAT?! Cheek! And THEN she even had the nerve to say: "Genuine affection isn't something you generate from a sneaky kiss on the back seat of the bus. Your father and Mary really felt for one another." "Well, why did she DUMP him, then?" I hissed. Some people on the next table turned their heads. "Why did she many Tom instead of HIM?"

Uh-oh, icicles from the nose time or what? I thought she'd march me straight from the shop and sell me to the nearest passer-by or something. But as usual, she stayed dead calm. A waitress came past with a fancy cake trolley. Mum stopped her and ordered us both a meringue. "What's this for?" I said when the waitress had gone. Mum flicked out a napkin and covered her lap. 'Well, I could attempt to be terribly witty and say it's to take the sour taste from your mouth, but I suppose that's something of a forlorn hope."

I hung my head and glared at the thing: a great big strawberry in an oyster-shell of cream. I felt a lot like a strawberry then. I don't like falling out with Mum. "I'm sorry," I muttered. "I should think so," she said. "You and that boy (tch! *that boy*) have caused an awful lot of ructions with your snooping around. Parents have a right to their privacy, Annabelle, just as much as you pair do." "Yes, Mum," I sighed, and stabbed my meringue.

We ate in silence for a bit after that. Then she looked up and her gaze seemed to soften. She must have been staring at the locket cos she said, "All right, as I've made you an honorary adult I'll tell you what really happened back then. But I don't want it broadcast all over Oxfordshire or gossiped about in the back row of the classroom, you understand? I'm not even sure you should share it with Guy, though I suppose he has just as much right to know." "Know what?" I said, pouting a bit. She broke off a piece of meringue with her fork. "That your father begged Mary to marry him once."

At that point the strawberry slithered out of my mouth, hit the edge of the table and squidged to the floor.

"Hmm," Mum went "that's exactly how I felt at the time: slack-jawed." "But . . . when?" I burbled, gaping like a fish. Mum dabbed her mouth with a napkin and said, "Mary and Tom hit a rocky patch once when she was two months pregnant with Guy.

Tom was away a lot on business and your father, then a humble lecturer at Warwick, got wind of their problems and made a rather naïve, last-ditch effort to win her, when really all she wanted was a shoulder to cry on." "But . . . that's *terrible*," I said. "How can he ask someone who's having someone else's baby to *marry him*? What about you?" She shrugged and twiddled her fork in the air. "Oh, I did what I always did in moments of exasperation with Franklin: entrenched myself in a hole in the ground. Underneath Hadrian's Wall, I think."

I sat up and set my shoulders straight. I couldn't believe what I was hearing. "You should have stuck him under Hadrian's Wall," I growled, "and piled some extra rocks on top!" She glanced to one side and nodded slightly as if she wished she'd thought of that at the time – and then she said this: "What you have to understand, is that in those days my relationship with your father was largely physical –" "Mu-um?" I hissed, looking around. "I could never quite reach him on the same emotional level that Mary had. I suppose he thought of her as a sort of soul-mate. Nevertheless I loved him deeply, and believed, deep down, he felt the same about me. But I knew things couldn't last the way they were unless I could get some commitment from him. So I took the most awful risk."

She paused to eat a bit of meringue. "Go on," I hissed, looking round the café. "Mum, you can't stop there!" She had a sip of coffee that seemed to take hours. Then at last she said, "Just before I left for Hadrian and his wall, I gave Franklin an ultimatum. I told him if he wasn't waiting for me at Warwick station when I returned from the dig, he and I were finished – for good." "Was he?" I said (which was a bit of a stupid question really because, well, I'm here, aren't I?) But my heart nearly burst when she actually replied: "No, he was in a prison cell."

A prison cell? Guy, you could have popped a tennis ball in my gob right then.

"Hmm," she nodded. "I'd told him which weekend I was coming back, but I'd forgotten to say which day. For two nights he slept rough on a bench on the platform in case I'd caught an early train. The police thought he was a vagrant and arrested him when he wouldn't move on. Fortunately, he managed to yell a message to the station porter who put up a banner for 'Mary Jane from York'. I saw the banner and went to bail him out. It was quite romantic really, sitting in the foyer of Warwick police station, cradling a cup of lukewarm tea. He told me I stank of stale northern mud. I told him he just stank. He admitted he'd been an absolute idiot – then said he wanted a child and would I be interested in helping him towards one later that night?" "Oh, Mum!" I exclaimed, but she carried straight on "We declared our undying love for one another and decided if this relationship was ever going to work we had to start with a totally clean sheet and confess our deepest sins . . ."

A few people heard that and started to whisper. "Mum," I cringed, "can't we leave the steamy bits out of it?" "You wanted to know," she said. "Anyway, I'm in the swing of it now."

And she was.

Guy, if you think its pretty embarrassing so far, you haven't heard anything yet. I nearly slid beneath the table when she started on this: she said Dad confessed that he'd always carried a torch for your mum and thought he probably always would. Well, we knew that, didn't we? But *then* she said – are you ready for this? – that was OK by her because she'd always fancied the pants off Tom!

At that point I scrunched through a bit of meringue and part of it skidded across the café floor.

"Oh, come on," Mum said. "Don't give me that 'Little Miss Innocent' look. I saw Guy at Mary's funeral. He's his father's son, all right. Very fanciable." I gave her such a hard stare that the temperature in the café dropped several degrees. "Mum! You can't fancy GUY! That's indecent!" She gave me what Ms Spence calls "a wistful smile". "All I meant was that if I were your age, I'd fancy him like mad."

Well, I couldn't argue with that. But then she ruined it totally by saying: "I wonder if he's got his father's feet? He always had lovely big feet, Tom Woodham. I do like whopping great feet on a man."

Yes. Thank you, Mother. Let's leave *onkeybats* out of it, shall we? (Oh, by the way, comparing smelly feet in the lounge, Guy Woodham, definitely qualifies as a disgusting habit – especially if it's done in the daytime. I think you should know I nearly heaved.)

So I changed the subject a bit and said, "Mum, if Dad was, y'know, *close* to Guy's mum, why didn't he go to her funeral? Didn't he want to say good-bye?" She tilted her head and let her gaze sweep out towards the spires again. "Oh, he wanted to go," she said, "but simply couldn't bring himself to do it. He didn't think he could face Tom again, not in such difficult circumstances." "But *you* went," I said, making it sound like a question. "Oh yes," she said. "As the villain of the piece, I felt I had to. Has Guy told you how we drifted apart?" I nodded. "Because of Alexander." Mum nodded sadly. "Mary spoke about him in that letter, you know – Alexander, I mean. How she wished things could have been different and how if we could only turn back the clock we'd all realize how much we could have gained from staying together."

I felt a bit weepy then. Mum reached out and squeezed my hand. "It was unfinished business, A. I had to be near her, one more time. Do you know what Mary's biggest regret was?" I shook my head. "Never seeing you."

That did it. "Oh," I went and shoved a cream-blodged napkin into my face. Mum tutted and pulled a few strands of my hair out of the mess. "She said in her letter that it would have been fascinating to see how you and Guy would have got along – that's sort of what started your digital tête-à-têtes." "I know," I snuffled. "Guy told me his mum introduced us." Mum smiled and waited while I blew my nose. "Hmm, rather belatedly though. It wouldn't have done to have launched you at Guy right away." "Oh *thanks!*" I snorted. "When did you decide to 'launch' me then?" "If you keep your voice down, I'll tell you," she said.

I kept my voice down.

"After the funeral, I managed to get a few quiet moments with Tom. I told him most of what Mary had said and that I thought she'd like us to keep in touch. He agreed. So over the next few months Tom and I exchanged the odd letter and card and even met up a couple of times." I butted in then and blurted out about the ram-headed sphinx card and how we thought that "Jane" and your dad were, well, at it. "Don't be ridiculous," she said. "I was offering an old friend emotional support. There were no heaving bodies involved whatsoever." "Oh, Mu-um," I went, batting my fists.

An elderly couple got up just then and frowned at Mum as they left the café.

She said, "Annabelle, nothing ever happened between me and Tom Woodham and nothing ever will. I'm telling you this in case you and your partner-in-crime decide to go off on another of your fantastic who-spawned-who journeys. For your information, I'm not planning any torrid affairs with Tom, Dick, Harry, Larry, Achmed or otherwise. I love your paranoid, barmy father. He's more than enough man for any woman to cope with. Now, where was I – before you sidetracked me with all this sex talk?"

I winced and reminded her about you and me e-mailing one another.

"Oh yes," she said. "By Christmas, Tom and I were on a pretty good footing. He was beginning to ask openly about your father then, but like most men in an emotional situation didn't think he should be the one to make the first move. So, one night, while your father was slightly off-guard after a couple of festive brandies, I persuaded him to give Tom a call. He wasn't entirely happy about it, but as it happened he had the perfect excuse. We had just lost our accountant, and Tom seemed like an ideal replacement. I wouldn't say it was the most fluent of calls, but they managed to string it out for the best part of an hour. Tom talked an awful lot about Guy and was clearly very worried about him.

Guy was seriously depressed and the bereavement counselling didn't seem to be helping. Then, to your father's eternal credit, he remembered Mary's hints about bringing the pair of you together and suggested to Tom that you might be better 'therapy' for Guy. And that was when I had a bright idea. I scribbled our e-mail address on a scrap of paper and shoved it under Franklin's nose. Tom prodded Guy – and, well, here we are a few months later, confessing all in a coffee shop in Oxford."

And that was that. So in a funny sort of way, they ALL introduced us – even Franklinstein, who I suppose I will have to make it up with now. Well, he did cuddle you at least – just keeping you warm until I came along!

My tummy's rumbling. Gotta go.

Neeowww . . . dumph!

(That was me launching myself at you – and landing!) Don't forget you're supposed to be phoning me tonight (who cares if my ear lobes do disintegrate).

Bye-ee, Fizzy (ha ha)
xxx

PS Rocket says n-n-ny-eh. He's sitting on top of the PC monitor.

THE CAVERNER ROAD PANCAKE DAY CATASTROPHE

Dear Rocket (I mean you!),

I felt such a nerd when your Mum picked the phone up. I mean, all the things I know about her now. And all the things she knows about me, including how I made you believe she wasn't really your Mum . . .

It was enough to get my tongue tied up in a reef knot, only she said, "Oh, Guy!" like she's known me for ages (I suppose she has, now I think about it) and started chatting away, and apologizing for you landing on the doorstep in the middle of the night (apologizing! as if I minded!) so that I thought she was never going to pass the phone over to you. She sounds just like an older version of you! You must have been trained as a marathon talker, starting when you were in nappies.

Anyway, I forgot to tell you this. I've finally found out! So just in case your Dad hasn't told you, here it is. Cue, flashback.

Place: Student house in Caverner Road.

Time: Back when they were all students, i.e. the Dark Ages. Pancake Day.

Cast: Mary Mary, Mary Jane, Franklin, Tom (the Caverner Road Four).

The Caverner-dwellers decided to have a pancake feast. None of them had ever made pancakes before and it was harder than they thought. It was a team effort. Mary Jane did the shopping and squeezed the lemons; Tom mixed the batter; Mary Mary did the frying and tossing; Franklin rolled up the pancakes and sprinkled the sugar and kept them warm under the grill. (Don't ask why it didn't occur to them to use a warm oven. Honestly, I wonder whether they were fit to be left alone in a house. Good job our generation's got more sense.)

Between them, they managed to make three pancakes – a bit mangled, Dad said, crispy in some places and soggy in others, but still fairly edible. And then it happened.

The frying pan was starting to stick, and Mary Mary had trouble tossing the last pancake. After she'd had a few goes, Franklin wanted to take over. He was convinced he'd be the best Pancake Tosser in the Known Universe. So he started tossing and flipping it and even trying back flips and double-twist somersaults and the occasional triple lutz. And while everyone was watching and clapping and picking bits of burnt batter off the floor, the pancakes under the grill got forgotten . . .

You've guessed. Next minute, there was a smell of burning, and flames burst out from the grill. Mary Mary and Mary Jane kept calm, and tried to simply lift the grill pan up and take it to the sink, but Franklin panicked. He grabbed Mary Mary's felt hat, which she'd left on top of the fridge, and started bashing at the flames with it. Soon the kitchen was full of the smell of charred hat, as well. So my dad chucked the contents of the washing-up bowl, including a few greasy spoons, all over your Dad and the hat, and they all ended up in fits of laughter clearing up the mess and eating toast instead.

But next Saturday, Franklin offered to buy my Mum a new hat and he took her into town to choose one. And they spent ages before coming back with an absolutely gorgeous hat (Dad says it's called a "cloche", which means bell, because that's the shape, and it's red with a felt rose on one side, and it made Mum look really beautiful like a thirties film star, and she wore it right up till last winter and it's still upstairs with her things), and my Dad says that's when he realized there was still SOMETHING between them, Franklin and Mum. And that's when he started being jealous of Franklin. And he couldn't believe his luck when Mum chose him, after all.

So I suppose you could tell your Dad that Mum still wore his hat, if it would make him happy. But if he ever offers to make pancakes, think very carefully before you accept.

About the coffee-shop soul-baring: they've been a bit devious, haven't they, our parents? If I'd known there was a guided missile heading my way, I'd have run a mile. I'm glad I didn't.

From the Landing Zone,
Guy
:* :* :* :* :*

WOW! GET THIS!

Dear Big Feet,

I have got something FANTASTIC to tell you – but you're not having it yet and you're not allowed to go to the end of this e-mail to find out either. If you do I will turn into your UGLY SISTER! So be warned. Do you promise? On your hairy onkeybats? OK read on. But remember, I'll be watching!

You know I said I had to make it up with Dad? Well, he wasn't in when we got home from town and still wasn't when I'd finished my coffee-shop message. I tried to grab him last night before you phoned, but he had some swanky college thing to go to and I was in bed by the time he came in.

Anyway, this morning I was reading your message about pancakes and hats (nice, I LOVE hats) when I heard him clomping about, moaning about "certain people" hogging the computer. So I dashed downstairs to find him. He was sitting in the lounge, reading a paper, resting his feet on the television stool. He grunted when he saw me and flapped his paper. I hooked one finger over the top and pulled it down a bit. "What?" he said, raising his eyes. I gave him my sweetest petal-like smile. "Don't mind me," I said. "I'm just doing an anthropology lesson."

Then I knelt down and whipped off his slippers and socks!

He banged his paper down. "Annabelle," he growled, "WHAT are you doing?" "Don't move, I'm checking your onkeybats," I said. "My *what*?" he said. "Your poddies," I explained (that's what civilized people call feet). Then I told about the Woodham Foot Appreciation Society and he groaned and said, "For goodness' sake. What do I have to do to prove I am your natural father?" I perched on his knee and put my arms around his neck. "You can tell me where I get my gorgeous looks from." And I *know* he was desperate to burst out laughing, but somehow he managed to keep a straight face. "I could also flip you over," he threatened. I swung my legs and said a bit cheekily, "I'll set my boyfriend on you if you do." "Charming," he said with a click of his tongue. "I introduce you to the boy of your dreams and you use him as a weapon against me."

Ha! Cheek or what!

So I smacked his chest. "Dad, don't fib. You know that Mary Mary introduced us, really." And this twitchy little smile broke out on his lips and he held up his hands like a prisoner, surrendering. "That's it," he said. "I give up. I should have known it's impossible to keep anything from you." "Yep," I said with a flick of my hair. "Mum told me *everything*. I even know about Warwick and how you asked Guy's mum to marry you once."

He winced and said something under his breath, but at least he seemed relieved that the truth was out. He twiddled a strand of my hair in his fingers, like he used to when I was a real little girl, and said: "I loved Guy's mother very much, Annabelle. I won't try to hide that from you. Sometimes, when I'm deep into this –" he held up the Wilfred Owen book – "I wonder what it would have been like . . . with her. Sharing her life . . . having a child with her. And then I think of you, my feisty little firebrand, and I remind myself how lucky I am. Not just to have a beautiful, gifted daughter, but a quite extraordinary wife as well – who, believe it or not, I adore."

I bit my lip and didn't know what to say. "Promise me you're not going to do any more silly disappearing tricks?" I gave a little shrug. "Not this week," I said. "I need two lifts to drama class." He smiled and slipped a hand around my waist. "That's better. Is this nonsense really all done?"

And as soon as he said that this wicked temptation leapt into my mind. "Nearly," I quipped. "Only nearly?" he frowned. I gave a solemn nod. "Jupiter's out of his cage again. I think he's *really* under the boards this time." Guy, it was brilliant;

his face turned the colour of an uncooked pancake. "Oh no!" he gasped. "When? How? I thought I'd fixed the latch last t –" And he broke off then cos he caught me snickering. "Got you!" I laughed, beating his chest. "Hmph," he went – and grabbed my wrists. "Yes, madam," he said, "and I've got YOU!"

And then he *did* flip me over! The horrible brute!

"You (smack) are the most precocious (smack) child I have ever (smack) known," he said. (Actually, it was more like tap, tap, tap; he's never hit me, ever; he was only playing. It didn't hurt, of course, but I squealed to good dramatic effect! Ms Spence would have been very impressed.) "But Dad, I'm the *only* precocious child you've ever known!" I protested. "And cheeky with it too," he said (smack).

Just then, Mum walked in and waltzed across the room as if NOTHING was happening! "Have you seen my glasses, Franklin?" she said. "Mu-um?" I shouted. "Dad's being cruel and horrible to me!" Dad said, "They were on the hall shelf last time I saw them." "Ah," she said, and went out again, letting Ginger run in "Ginger, my angel, protect me!" I shouted. He slobbered my face. Great. Just what you need when you're getting your come-uppance – dog slobber running all down your nose!

"Now listen to me, young lady," Dad whispered, giving me a gentle poke in the ribs. "I've got something important to tell you." "What?" I said. Ginger went woof and Dad tapped me again for not keeping the dog under control!!! "I'm taking your mother away at Easter, but it's a secret and I don't want her to know about it yet."

I thought, Great, here's my chance to blackmail him! "What's it worth to you?" I shouted.

(Bad mistake. He started tickling me, then!)

"No!" I squealed. "Well, pay attention then," he said. "I thought we'd go walking in the Peak District, OK?" I flapped my legs in disappointment. "Oh, thanks," I moaned. "Go to the Peak District and leave me on my own with a mad dog and a sore bum, won't you? I'll be perfectly all right. Thanks a bunch!" Then he said, "When I said 'we', I meant . . . the four of us." At the risk of not being able to sit down for a week I said, "Dad, you've gone sea-lion, there's only three of us." "Not if we invite someone else," he said. "You mean Laura?" I said. "No-oo!" he tutted and gave me a smack for being dumb! "Who would you most like to go on holiday with?" "GUY?!!" I screamed. "Keep your voice down," he hissed, prodding my back "You'll have to make sure he asks Tom's permission."

No problemo! Hand me the mobile!

"Aw, Dad!" I cried. "I really really love you! I really, really, really, really, really, REALLY love you." He roared with laughter and tickled me again. "Good,

I'm delighted to hear it."

SMACK!

See what I put up with for you, Guy Woodham? Oh please say yes. Oh please, please, please. Mail me, phone me, send a pigeon if you like. Just say YES!!!

Yee! I'm so happy. I don't know what to do – ring Laura, or cry, or both. Both, I think. Talk about, "If there's anything that you want . . .?" A holiday. Together. Yeeeeeeeeeeeesss!

Mad about you,
A
PS :* x loads

MORE ABOUT THAT RAT

Dear Annabelle,

As soon as I put the phone down just now I remembered the things I forgot to tell you. That always happens.

Well, it's bound to, really, cos you talk so much I can hardly get a word in . . . e-mail still has its uses.You can't interrupt me! So nyah! (And Ny-eh to Rocket!)

I'm really glad you're so pleased about the hat. When I told you, there was such a long silence that I thought we'd been cut off. Then this ear-blasting shriek! I honestly thought you were being attacked – by a combined force of Jupiter, Ginger, your Dad, Darth Vader, Inspector Morse and the total Oxford police force. It took me a few seconds to realize it was a yell of delight. It nearly perforated my eardrum – I'm still a bit deaf in that ear as a matter of fact, but don't worry, I'll probably get over it. And then you took so long telling me how you'll wear it in bed, in the shower, in the Peak District and in the swimming-pool (you won't really, will you?) that I forgot to tell you all this.

I asked if I could get Mum's hat from the top of the wardrobe. Dad came up with me and took it out of its box. There it was, the red hat, shaped to Mum's head. There was even a stray black hair inside it, clinging to the felt. Suddenly I had a picture of Mum wearing this hat, laughing and happy. For a minute I thought we were going to need another loo roll (and supplies are desperately short now) but then Dad plonked it on my head and said, "Look at yourself in the mirror! It quite suits you." Of course I looked like a total prat – this elegant hat with my jeans and fleece and trainers – so I started mincing about and we both ended up in fits.

Then Dad said, "What made you want it, anyway?" I didn't really know, but all of a sudden the idea popped into my head. And at exactly the same moment, Dad said. "I suppose you want to give it to Annabelle, don't you?"

So I sat down on the bed and thought about it. Would it be wrong? Shouldn't Dad keep it? But then I thought of Franklin buying the hat for Mum, and Mum wanting us to get together, and suddenly it all seemed right.

Dad had gone all serious too. He sat down next to me, and he took the hat back and put it on his lap and stroked it, like it was a cat, with his elbows stuck out as if I was going to snatch it from him. Then he said, "Yes. I think it's a really good idea. It sort of – seals things. And Annabelle will look great in it" So I said, "Are you sure? I mean, it's Mum's hat. Don't you want to keep it?"

He thought a bit more, and then he shoved it at me as if he might still change his mind. Then he said, "Yes, I do. But I think you should give it to Annabelle. As long as Jane won't be upset? After all, it's Franklin's gift to Mum. She might not want to be reminded of that."

So I said, I didn't think your Mum would be upset. Because Mum was her friend too, wasn't she? Anyway, your Mum sounds like a really feisty lady. I said that to Dad, and he smiled and said, "Oh, she's THAT all right." I nearly said, Do you know she fancied the pants off you once? But then I thought, well, if he knew, he knew, and if he didn't, there's not much point telling him now. There've been enough complications, haven't there?

She sounds great, your Mum. I can just imagine her dragging your Dad up Kinder Scout and the White Peak. But I hope she's forgiven me for my daft theories, cos she doesn't sound like someone I'd like to get on the wrong side of.

I still haven't told you about the end of *The Winter's Tale*, have I? I didn't want to, before, because this is how it goes.

Perdita comes back to her father, and they're all happy, except for one thing – she reminds everyone of Hermione, who died years ago. And they all go off to look at a fantastic statue of Hermione, made by this famous sculptor. Everyone stands there looking at it in wonder, because it's so lifelike. Life-size. It looks as if it's about to speak. It even seems to have got older! And then this magical music starts up and they all stand there mesmerized, and the statue starts to move and it comes to life.

It really is Hermione.

She comes down from the plinth thing and she puts her arms round her husband's neck. She's not dead after all. Now she's reunited with her husband and her long-lost daughter. It's like a fairy-tale ending.

I know that's not going to happen. There isn't a statue of my Mum, and if there was, it wouldn't come to life. This isn't a fairy-tale, it's real. When I watched that video, I thought, just for one idiotic second: Suppose Mum isn't really dead? Suppose she comes back?

But that was stupid. She isn't coming back. She never will.

All the same, I know now that my Dad loved her and that your Dad loved her. And I loved her. And she'll never be forgotten. And that must mean her life was worth something, wasn't it?

So I do want to give you my Mum's hat. I'm going to pack it up really carefully and put it in the post tomorrow. Registered Post, Dad said – it's too precious to get lost in some sorting office.

And he's right – you will look great in it. I can't wait to see you wearing it. In fact I just can't wait to see you.

Guy

:* x 100

WISHING YOU WERE HERE

Dear Yunk,

The hat arrived this morning. It's BRILLIANT! The very best present I've EVER had. (Oops, well, the equal very best present I've ever had as I now own a precious family locket and a fantastic kitten and a personal CD player – oh, you know what I mean.) It (the hat) is just a weeny bit big and keeps slipping down over my eyes at the moment. Mum has offered to pin it for me, but Dad keeps telling her she shouldn't bother as my head is sure to swell more than enough to accommodate the slack once I start "cat-walking" in front of my pals.

Ha, ha.

:P to him.

And a bit of a :P to Ms Spence as well. Bet you never thought you'd hear me say *that*. I've gone right off Mizz S just lately. Yesterday I told her what you said on the phone, about us doing *The Winter's Tale* for our next school play. "Super suggestion, Annabelle!" she gushed. "Hermione is one of my favourite parts. Of course to remain so statuesque, to be the absolute pinnacle of audience attention, demands extraordinary grace and courage. It requires an actress with great stage presence to really capture Hermione properly." She clasped her hands to her chest and beamed: "Oh yes, I can see it now! I can see TRACEY, atop the plinth!" Atop the plinth? Atop the *plinth*? I felt like saying, "Are you sure the stage won't crumble under her weight?"

I should have.

"But Ms Spence" I wailed. "*I*'m Hermione!" "Oh no," she said, flapping her hands, "I picture you as . . . a shepherdess cavorting in the country dance . . ."

Well, she can go and cavort right off! I don't think I want to be in her drama group any more. I am going to take up poetry instead. Poetry's not bad when you get going, is it? I've just finished one called *The Onkeybat Cave*, which is all about enormous socks! "Remarkably surreal" was how Ms Spence described it. She says I have a "jewelled mind" and must continue to explore its "innermost reaches". There. Never knew I had a jewelled mind with reaches, did you?

Bet Mr Phiggins does. He thinks I'm a genius. At the beginning of every Maths lesson he sets us a little arithmetic problem and gives a prize to the first one to solve it. Last Thursday he said, "If it costs ninety pence per mile to travel in a taxi from here to Hereford, how much would the final fare be, approximately?" I got it to the nearest twenty pence! Bit of a cheat, of course, but I wasn't going to let on how I knew, was I? The prize was a little carton of juice. I drank it down to the dregs at break and shook the rest over Stinkler's head when he came past with his Walkman on. It was brilliant.

Anyway, I'm going off the subject (as usual). Please say a MONSTER thank you to your dad and tell him I will cherish my new cloche ALWAYS. Tell him it will never see a pancake or a flaming grill, ever. And I think you should advise him to buy some tissues because he might just go all weepy again when he sees the attached photo.

Say thanks to Mary Jane and her digital camera! Chee-se!

The gorgeous Annacloche (geddit?)

:* x the Universe (it knows what it's doing).

PS Have you bought that foot deodorant yet? I am not going to the Peak District with you until I have seen clear evidence of a receipt.

A FULL AND FRANK GUIDE TO THE DISGUSTING HABITS OF GUY WOODHAM
(in no particular order)

Annabelle, Guy told me you'd asked for this list, but he was too much of a coward. "I can't *tell* her, can I?" he said. "It'll put her off me for good." But I think you should be warned, so I'm doing it on his behalf. Are you sure you want to know?

OK, read on –

- Leaving a mulch of socks on his bedroom floor.
- Stealing *my* socks when he runs out, because none of his have made it to the washing-machine.
- Making the most excruciatingly awful pasta meals (sorry, Guy, I know you do try) and forcing me to eat them.
- Humming along (tunelessly) to his Walkman when I'm trying to watch TV.

- Grinding his teeth when he's asleep and dreaming.
- Mashing all his shepherd's pie into a big heap with peas and gravy, then eating it.
- Hiding school newsletters in the bottom of his rucksack along with mouldy chocolate remnants and fossilized apples.
- Eating mayonnaise on toast, with strawberry jam (don't ask me what made him even try it).
- Hogging the computer to send endless e-mails to a certain Miss Annabelle King.
- (Last few days.) Running up a huge phone bill, ditto.
- Leaving his trainers strategically scattered where I'm bound to fall over them.
- Trying to shave with my razor (and a magnifying glass) and then pretending it was someone else who left my stuff all over the bathroom.
- Leaving toe-nail clippings on the bathroom carpet (a major threat to sensitive onkeybats).
- Washing up so hopelessly that you can still recall what you were eating two days before – there are remnants of it left on the cutlery.
- Shoving everything in the known universe under his bed: his version of "tidying his room".

- Eating pistachio nuts in bed and getting shells in the duvet.

Sorry, but you did ask!

Please don't let any of it put you off. He's really a very nice Guy. And crazy about you.

Tom Woodham

– Guy's on his way upstairs now, so sending this before he stops me –

My Guy

by Annabelle Hermione King

you're my Shakespeare sonnet
my Wilfred, my Owen
my ordinary someone
my best A*

you're my tough guy
my summit
my points of the compass
my west-north-west
my border boy

you're my rugby tackle
my Last Mohican
my yero, my yeart-throb
my long-distance
yunk

always with me
(though I never see you)
whispering to me
(though I never hear your voice).
I know you're there
in the ether, all around me
like the comfort of a warm wind

touching my heart.

KLANG BIN ELENA
4
YUG HAWMOOD

THE
(d'Lacey)
END
(Newbery)

Chris d'Lacey says of Linda Newbery . . .

I think Linda is a terrific writer. It scared me to death when she first suggested collaboration because I feared J. could never match the beauty of her prose. She has written lots of books covering various age group. My personal favorites are *Ice Cat* for younger readers and *The Nowhere Girl* for young adults, which was nominated for the Carnegie Medal. Linda is a chatty, amiable person and a good friend. She loves cats, vegetarian food, and tending her garden pond. I'd like to think we might write together again. It would be interesting to see how the relationship between Guy and Annabelle develops.

Linda Newbery says of Chris d'Lacey...

I didn't know Chris d'Lacey when I was asked to judge a short-story competition and chose his (anonymous) entry as the winner. It wasn't just the best – it was outstandingly the best. Chris is good at winning prizes – his first novel, *Fly, Cherokee, Fly*, was Highly Commended for the Carnegie Medal. If you want to read the best description of a pigeon you're ever likely to come across, go to page 130. Chris lives with his wife, Jay, his cat, Pippa, and five pigeons, and knows all about confocal microscopy. He is a tireless e-mailer and a generous friend, and tells terrible jokes.

OTHER BARN OWL TITLES YOU MIGHT ENJOY

THE DEVIL'S ARITHMETIC

by Jane Yolen

£5.99 ISBN 1-903015-18-8

A moving and exciting book that gives a very personal account of the Holocaust that is both realistic and uplifting.

Hannah is very reluctant to visit her grandparents in New York for the annual Passover meal, she is bored with hearing about her grandfather's grim wartime experiences. However when Hannah opens the door to her grandparents' flat, she finds herself not in their comfortable and safe home but in Poland in 1943.

Gradually Hannah realises that she is with her own family and she wants to stop the inevitable happening but knows that she can not stop history. Rounded up by the Germans and taken to a camp, Hannah discovers unexpected depths in herself and a different understanding of her family.

Written by Jane Yolen, one of the most respected of American writers.

"This is an intelligent, imaginative and original perspective on events of which today's children need to be reminded. I couldn't put it down." *Adèle Geras*

A QUESTION OF COURAGE

by Marjorie Darke

£5.99 ISBN 1-903015-21-9

When young seamstress Emily Palmer sets off on her very first bike ride she has no idea that her whole life is about to be changed. On that ride Emily encounters her first suffragette and decides to devote her life to the cause of Votes for Women.

In pursuit of what she believes Emily leaves her family, her work and her town but as time goes on, while she never questions the justice of her cause, she begins to worry about the violent aspects of the campaign. After a spell in prison, Emily finds the courage to speak out, not only against her enemies but also against her friends. In the midst of all this turbulence Emily experiences love for the first time.

"The sheer breadth of the canvas, the unsentimental exactness of observation, the taut style, the distinct lack of fudging of difficult issues of conduct and relations are all superb." *The School Librarian*

THE GATHERING

by Isobelle Carmody

£5.99 ISBN I-903015-09-X

When Nat moves to Cheshunt with his mother he hopes for a better life. However there is something wrong with the town, everyone is too well behaved, the crime rate is too low, someone is controlling the population and it seems to be the head of the school in partnership with the police.

Nat and his new friends and a strange ghostly girl feel compelled to oppose the sinister power that dominates the town and discover that a loyal group can achieve things that one person cannot.

A very exciting and compelling book by one of Australia's most popular writers.

"This is a wonderful and intelligent book – I found it impossible to put down." *Michael Rosen*

SOME OTHER WAR

by Linda Newbery

£5.99 ISBN 1-903015-20-0

Twins, Alice and Jack Smallwood are approaching their eighteenth birthdays when the First World War breaks out. Both twins work for the wealthy Morland family, Jack as a groom in the stables and Alice as a chambermaid, but the War catapults both of them into new and unimagined worlds. Jack goes into the trenches and Alice becomes a nurse. While the newspapers report heroic victories,brother and sister see the grimmer reality. The narrative, alternating between the two characters, gives both a male and a female perspective on the drastic events and tragic losses that were so particularly terrible in that conflict.

Some Other War is a moving and compassionate story of young people trying to maintain their integrity, courage and sense of purpose under the most testing of circumstances.

Linda Newbery has been nominated twice for the Carnegie Prize, most recently for *The Shell House*, another book that uses World War I as its subject.

"One of the most powerful recreations of the Great War that I have encountered. A riveting read!" *Mary Hoffman*